VLAD *the* DRAC

DOWN UNDER

VLAD the DRAC
DOWN UNDER

ANN JUNGMAN

Illustrated by George Thompson

Collins

An imprint of HarperCollinsPublishers

First published in Great Britain by Collins in Young Lions in 1989
This edition published by Collins in 1997
Collins is an imprint of HarperCollins *Publishers* Ltd
77-85 Fulham Palace Road, Hammersmith, London, W6 8JB

1 3 5 7 9 8 6 4 2

Text copyright © Ann Jungman 1989
Illustrations copyright © George Thompson 1989

ISBN 0 00 673613 0

The author asserts the moral right to be
identified as the author of the work.

Printed and bound in Great Britain by Caledonian International
Book Manufacturing Ltd, Glasgow G64

For Meg, Morag and Eileen

1
HIJACKED!

The Stone family were sitting in the café at London Airport sipping drinks and munching cream cakes.

'Mmm,' said Dad, through a mouthful of cream, 'things couldn't have worked out better. We escape from England and spend two months in the sun, just when everyone else is getting ready to freeze all winter.'

'What I'm looking forward to is lying on a beach in the sun,' agreed Mum dreamily.

'I'm a bit sad to be missing Christmas at home,' confessed Judy. 'I really like Christmas.'

'They have Christmas in Australia, silly,' Paul reminded her.

'I know, but it's not the same in the sun. It just won't feel like a proper Christmas.'

'We'll go down to the beach for Christmas,' said Mum, 'and eat turkey sandwiches on the beach.'

'It sounds fantastic,' said her son enthusiastically. 'I can't wait to get there.'

'Yes, all in all,' continued Dad, stretching out contentedly, 'things couldn't have worked out better. Just when we're all completely worn out from having Vlad to stay at the same time as the new baby arrived, along comes my chance to go to Australia as second violin with the New Philharmonic Orchestra. And what's more, there are absolutely no vampires in Australia; the climate doesn't suit them. Yes, things have definitely turned out very well indeed.'

No sooner had he finished speaking than a familiar voice hailed them:

'Judy, Paul, Mum and Dad, h-e-l-l-o!! Well, fancy meeting you here. And the Snoglet. What a lovely surprise. I've just been trying to phone you. This explains why I didn't get a reply.'

The Stone family sat round the table and stared at the tiny vampire in dismay. Dad went white.

'Hallo, Vlad,' he said, doing his best to sound jovial. 'We just came to meet some friends. Their plane has been delayed, so we were passing the time having some cake. What are you doing here, if I may ask?'

'Of course you may ask,' said Vlad smiling broadly. 'I'm on my way home from visiting Mal in California. I have to change planes, to get to Romania. I must say it's a very long flight; it's been over twelve hours since I left Mal's house and I'm tired.'

'It's called jet lag,' Judy told him. 'It's not only the long flight but you fly into a different time zone and it's hard to adapt.'

'Oh, I see,' said the vampire. 'Is that why I'm feeling so strange? Well, I'm sorry if I'm not my usual lively self, it must be this jet lag. Are you suffering from jet lag?' the vampire asked Dad. 'You don't seem very lively either.'

'Er, no,' said Dad quickly. 'It's not that, it's just that I'm worried about these friends who are so late.'

'If you're only meeting friends why have you got all that baggage with you?' demanded the vampire.

'It's not ours,' Dad assured him. 'We're looking after it for someone.'

'Dad!' exclaimed Judy. 'Stop telling Vlad fibs.'

'Judith,' said her father in a threatening tone.

'Well, why shouldn't Vlad know that we're going

11

off to Australia for a couple of months? Dad has got a job with an orchestra, Vlad, and he's going to tour Australia and we're going with him. Isn't that wonderful?'

'Australia?' exclaimed Vlad, looking horrified. 'That's terrible! You poor things. No wonder Dad didn't want me to know. Oh dear, poor old Stones, poor little Snoglet.'

'What's wrong with Australia?' demanded Paul indignantly.

'What isn't wrong with Australia?' replied Vlad contemptuously. 'It's on the other side of the world and everyone walks around upside down drinking beer while kangaroos jump up and down on them, *and* there isn't one single vampire there. I wouldn't go to Australia, not if you paid me. You have my sincere sympathies,' and he yawned loudly.

'Your views are very out of date, Vlad,' Dad told the vampire. 'Australia is a very exciting multicultural place, where all kinds of interesting things are happening and I hear that the scenery is amazing and that the flora and fauna are quite unique and utterly fascinating, so I think you should revise your ideas a bit.'

'He's gone, Nick,' said Mum soothingly. 'Vlad obviously didn't want to hear your defence of Australia.'

'That's just like him,' complained Dad. 'Never interested in hearing what anyone else has to say, always the same old boring prejudices. Still, if it succeeded in getting rid of him that's fine by me.'

'But, Dad,' interrupted Judy, 'I wanted to hear about Vlad's time in California with Mal and things.'

'Well, I didn't drive him away,' said her father. 'I wasn't rude or unfriendly, he just took himself off. Now come on, let's go into the departure lounge where Vlad won't be able to find us.'

'But, Dad, I want to say goodbye to Vlad and give him our address in Australia.'

'Judy,' said her mother, 'be reasonable, Vlad could be anywhere.'

'He's probably on a bus going to the terminal where the planes leave for Europe. He's got to catch a flight to Romania,' Dad said with relief.

'We really can't risk missing our plane to Australia while you go and look for Vlad,' said Mum firmly.

'He could at least have said goodbye,' said Judy tearfully.

'He was very jet lagged,' her mother pointed out, 'I expect he just forgot. Come on now, we'll send him a very special Christmas card from Australia.'

So the Stone family got out their passports and filed through to the departure lounge.

Half an hour later they were on the plane. An air hostess came over to help Mum with the baby's carrycot.

'I see your baby has got her toys with her,' said the air hostess smiling. 'Have a nice trip and do let us know if you need anything.'

They found their seats and Mum had one with plenty of room for the carrycot. After a while the aircraft took off and the Stones watched while the hostesses showed them the emergency drill. Paul yawned.

'I'm bored, Mum,' he complained. 'What can I do?'

'We've got well over twenty hours in the air,' Mum reminded him, 'so you'll have to keep yourself occupied. But there will be some films in a bit.'

'What films?' asked Paul, cheering up.

'Come on, now,' said Mum, 'don't be so helpless. Look, they're all listed in that magazine in front of you.'

Paul took it out and searched through to find

13

out which film was to be shown.

'Hey, Mum, Judy, guess what – *Marauding Monsters of the Outer Galaxy* is going to be on.'

'Oh no,' groaned Dad. 'No matter where I go I can't escape from that vampire.'

'Well, you don't have to watch it, Nick,' said Mum calmly. 'It's completely voluntary; just don't plug the earphones in.'

'That's all well and good,' griped Dad, 'but even if I don't listen to the sound track he'll still be up there on the screen in front of me in all his green horribleness.'

'Oh Nick, you're as bad as Paul. Now stop it. You can go to sleep while the film is on, or read a book, but don't carry on about it.'

Shortly after take-off they were all given some food and then Paul and Judy settled down to read their books until the film began. The baby woke up and began to cry. Mum lifted her out of her cot to comfort her. Suddenly, to her horror, she noticed a tiny green hand sticking out from under the baby's covers.

'Judy,' hissed Mum. 'Look!' and she pointed to the green hand. Judy went pale and pulled back the cover. There, sleeping peacefully, lay Vlad.

'Oh no!' whispered Judy. 'What are we going to do?'

'One of us will have to tell your father.'

'I'll do it,' sighed Judy. 'I'd better do it now before Vlad wakes up and Dad finds out anyway.'

'I'm going to change Zoe,' said Mum. 'Good luck.'

So while her mother went off, Judy leaned over and touched her father's arm.

'Dad,' she said nervously.

'Umm,' said her father, turning a page in his book.

'Dad, I've got something to tell you.'

14

Reluctantly her father shut his book.

'All right, Judy,' he said. 'I'm all ears: what is it?'

'Well, Dad, you know Vlad didn't say goodbye at the airport?'

'Yes,' agreed her father patiently.

'That's why,' she said, pointing to the carry cot.

'I can't bear it,' howled Dad, burying his head in his hands. 'I can't get away from him, not even when I get on a plane to go to the other side of the world. I was so looking forward to our time in Australia and now this. I'm a tolerant man, Judy, I never quarrel with anyone, but this is too much for flesh and blood to bear. You'll have to do something. You're his friend, you're the one who likes him, you decide what to do.'

'But, Dad, I don't have a clue what to do either!'

'What s going on?' asked Paul.

'Vlad fell asleep in Zoe's cot, look.'

Paul hooted with laughter.

'And Vlad was so sorry for us going to Australia. He will get a shock when he wakes up.'

'He's not coming to Australia with us,' declared Dad. 'He'll just have to get off the plane at the first stop we come to and get a plane back to Romania. We'd better tell one of the crew that they've got a stowaway on board. First we'd better wake Vlad up. Judy, since you like Vlad so much I declare you the vampire waker-upper-in-chief.'

'Oh, all right,' sighed Judy. 'Here goes. Vlad, Vlad, wake up.'

The little vampire sat up and rubbed his eyes.

'Where am I?' he said.

'You're on the plane to Australia,' Judy explained. 'You fell asleep in Zoe's cot.'

'On the way to Australia!' shrieked the vampire. 'Do something! Don't just stand there looking gormless. Pull the emergency cord! Anything! Just get them to turn round. I do not want to go to Australia!'

An air hostess came running over.

'Is there a problem?' she asked.

'A problem!' declared Vlad. 'There most certainly is a problem, I have been hijacked. I was on my way home to Romania to spend Christmas with my family and this man hijacked me.'

'Is this true, sir?' asked the hostess.

'No, it isn't,' shouted Dad. 'The last thing I want on a long plane journey is Vlad.'

'Vlad the Drac!' cried the air hostess. 'How extraordinary. We're showing your film on the plane.'

'Oh, really!' said Vlad. 'That shows a lot of sense on the part of the crew of this excellent machine. Now, madam, will you please tell the pilot to turn this plane around and take me back to London or I'll vampirise him.'

'We can't do that,' said the air hostess. 'We'll have to go on to our first destination, but you can get off there and go back to Romania. If they'll let a vampire off, that is.'

A tear ran down Vlad's cheek.

'But Mrs Vlad will be so worried. She promised to be at the airport with the five children to meet me and if I don't turn up she won't know what to think.'

'We'll send a message to Bucharest saying that you're on this plane, and someone will explain to your wife.'

'And I haven't got my luggage,' moaned the vampire, 'and all the presents for the children. They'll get lost.'

'No,' the hostess assured him. 'They'll get sent on to Romania and we'll make sure your wife gets them.'

'Poor old Vlad, poor little Drac,' complained the vampire. 'All I wanted to do was go home and now I'm on my way to Australia, of all places.'

'Don't worry so much,' said Judy soothingly. 'You'll get home a couple of days late, that's all, even if you have to come all the way to Sydney with us.'

'That's all! That's all!' exclaimed Vlad. 'It's all well and good for you to say that, it isn't you it's happening to. Honestly, Judy, you knew I was tired and jet lagged. Why didn't you check that I was all right?'

'We thought you'd just gone off,' Judy told him. 'I was all upset because you didn't say goodbye.'

'Well, I shall say goodbye to you loud and clear,' said Vlad sourly. 'As soon as possible. Australia indeed. What Mrs Vlad will say I tremble to think.'

'Can I get you something to eat?' asked the hostess. 'That might make you feel better.'

'Madam,' said Vlad irately, 'nothing, absolutely nothing in the world will make me feel better, except being returned to my destination without any more delay.'

Just then Mum came back from the toilet with the baby.

'We've got an extra passenger,' Dad told her grimly.

'Yes, I know,' said Mum. 'I saw him when I picked up the baby.'

'I fell asleep,' Vlad told her, ' 'cos I was jet lagged. This is the worst thing that ever happened to me. It's the end, I know it is, I'll never see my dear Magda and my little ones again. Hijacked to Australia. All I can say is, thank goodness Great Uncle Ghitza isn't here to see what is happening to me. He would die of shame. Whoever heard of a vampire in Australia?'

'I brought you a little something to eat, Vlad,'

said Mum soothingly, and she handed him a little bar of soap from the plane's bathroom.

'I'm not hungry,' moaned Vlad. 'I shall never eat again.'

But he peeled the paper off the bar of soap and began to nibble.

'Hey, this is good,' he said. 'Yummy. I'd better finish it up, just to maintain my strength. Are there any more like this?'

So Judy and Paul took it in turns to go to the toilet and stuff their pockets with the small bars of soap. Vlad munched his way through one after another as tears ran down his face.

After a while one of the hostesses spoke to the passengers over the intercom.

'Ladies and gentlemen, we will shortly be showing this evening's film *Marauding Monsters of the Outer Galaxy*. Before we begin, may we just say that some passengers seem to have been using soap rather generously and that we are in danger of running out, so could people please be a little more careful.'

Dad glared at Judy and Paul.

'All right, you two, I presume you're behind this soap business. Hand over what's left.'

Reluctantly Judy and Paul gave him the remaining bars of soap.

'There are a couple of hundred bars here,' said their father in an amazed tone.

'I'm jolly hungry,' complained Vlad. 'I'm eating to comfort myself and now you deprive me even of that. If I can't eat the airline's soap give me your shaving cream instead.'

'You go anywhere near my shaving cream,' said Dad grimly, 'and you will be ejected from this plane without a parachute. Now I'm going to return this soap to the hostess. Goodness knows what she'll think.'

So Dad returned all the soap bars and explained why the children had taken them.

'I'll go and see what else I can find for you, sir,' she told Vlad. 'We may have some of the powder that we use to clean the lavatories to spare.'

Vlad groaned. 'Now I'll have to starve as well. Oh well, at least there's one thing to be grateful for: things have hit rock bottom and they absolutely cannot get any worse. Poor old Vlad, poor little Drac.'

The hostesses went up and down the plane giving out earphones for the film. Then there was another announcement.

'Ladies and gentlemen. We are privileged to have on board this plane Vlad the Drac, one of the stars of the film. We hope very much that he might be willing to answer questions and sign autographs after the film.'

'You know,' said Vlad, brightening up, 'I think I may just manage to enjoy this flight after all. Can I sit on your knee, Judy, and watch me being wonderful in the film?'

'Course,' said Judy. 'I'd like that.'

The lights went down and the film began.

'There's no sound,' exclaimed Vlad. 'It's not a silent version, is it?'

'No,' Judy assured him. 'It's just that not everyone wants to watch the film, some people want to sleep or read, so you have special earphones for the sound.'

'You mean, there are people on this plane who would rather sleep or read than watch my film? I'll soon put a stop to that. Vampirising is too good for them, the callous, uncultured brutes.'

Judy kept a firm hold on Vlad. 'You just stay put. I won't have you flying round the plane pestering people.'

'But *I* want to hear the words, even if none of the other people do,' Vlad told her tearfully. 'Hostess, hostess, come here this minute, I need a set of earphones.'

'You don't shout at them like that,' said Judy blushing. 'You ring that bell there, at the side of the seat.'

'Well, how was I to know,' sniffed Vlad and he leaned on the bell till one of the hostesses came rushing up.

'Is something wrong?' she cried. 'Can I help in some way?'

'I most certainly hope so,' Vlad told her. 'What I need is a pair of earphones, so I can listen to the sound in the film.'

'Yes, of course, sir,' said the hostess. 'I'm so relieved it's nothing serious. You rang the bell so hard I thought someone was ill.'

'Oh no,' said Vlad casually. 'But my need for a pair of earphones is just as significant as some silly person getting ill. Now hurry up or the film will be half over before I get to hear one single word.'

The hostess brought the earphones; Vlad stared at them.

'I can't wear those,' he said. 'I've got a very small head.'

'I'm sorry, sir, but they only come in the one size.'

'Poor old Vlad, poor little Drac,' moaned the vampire. 'Everything done for people as usual.'

'Sit on my shoulder, Vlad,' suggested Judy. 'And share my earphones.'

'Humm,' sniffed the vampire. 'I'd have preferred a special Vlad-sized pair of my own, but I suppose this will have to do.'

When the film was over Vlad fell peacefully asleep

in Judy's lap till the air hostesses started to hand out more meals. Judy pulled down the tray in front of her to put her meal on.

'What's going on?' came a voice. 'I'm being squashed.'

Judy pulled Vlad out from underneath and sat him on the arm of her seat. Vlad looked at the woman next to him.

'I don't think you should be eating all this food,' he told her. 'All you've been doing is sitting down and watching a film, nothing to work up an appetite. Hostess, take that meal away. This lady isn't hungry.'

'Bring it back here!' yelled the woman. 'How dare you interfere! I'll decide if I'm hungry.'

Vlad gave her a long look.

'Madam,' he informed her, 'from the look of you, I would say you decide too often that you are hungry.'

'Don't take any notice,' Judy told the woman. 'Vlad's just upset because he wasn't planning on going to Australia. I'm very sorry he's being so rude.'

'Why don't you want to go to Australia?' asked the woman.

'If you don't know,' said Vlad loftily, 'there is no point in my telling you.'

'Vlad, will you stop being so rude,' snapped Judy.

'Well, I'm bored,' moaned the vampire. 'This flight is too long. Twenty-six hours – I can't bear it.'

'It's the same for all of us, Vlad. I'm bored too.'

'That's as may be, Judy, but vampire boredom is not like human boredom. It's a hundred times worse and I have got a very bad attack.'

'Why don't you go to sleep in Zoe's cot?' she suggested. 'There won't be any trays of food being passed around in there.'

'Humm,' sniffed Vlad. 'I suppose I'd better escape

from all these people. But I must clean my teeth first. That's vital.'

'Why is it vital?' asked the woman.

Vlad's eyes lit up. 'All the better to vampirise you with, my dear,' he said in a menacing tone.

'Vlad, stop it,' said Judy sharply. 'Just behave. Don't worry, he really is harmless, he just likes to act tough. I'll take him to the bathroom and put him in the baby's cot. He won't bother you any more, I promise.'

'Actually, I'm very tired,' Vlad told the woman. 'So I'll leave you alone for the moment. But don't get complacent: I may get vampirish later on.'

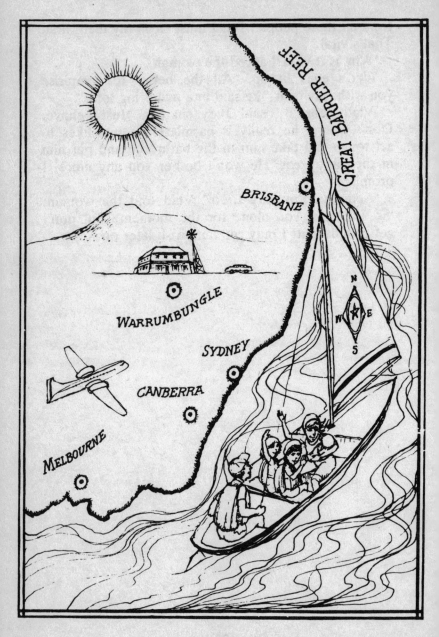

GREAT BARRIER REEF

BRISBANE

WARRUMBUNGLE

SYDNEY

CANBERRA

MELBOURNE

2

AUSTRALIA

Before the flight was over, Vlad signed everyone's menu as a souvenir of the flight they had shared with him. Then he went back to sleep in Zoe's cot.

As they approached Sydney Airport Dad said glumly to Judy, 'You'd better wake up your little friend so that he can explain to the immigration officer about what happened.'

Judy leaned over and shook Vlad.

'Go 'way,' he murmured sleepily, then rolled over and went back to sleep.

'Vlad,' said Judy firmly, 'we're going to arrive in Australia soon. You've got to wake up. You'll have

to explain who you are to the immigration people at the airport. As they wouldn't let you off the plane en route, you'll have to talk to the Australian authorities.'

Vlad sat up grumpily and rubbed his eyes.

'I shall not explain anything to anyone,' he informed Judy snootily. 'I shall merely insist on being put on the next flight back to Romania and no messing around or there'll be some vampirising done, I can tell you. Australia indeed. The end of the earth and upside down.'

Vlad was still complaining loudly when they landed.

'When are we going to get off this plane?' demanded Vlad. 'I must get on and arrange my journey home. I haven't got any time to shilly-shally and mess around.'

An air hostess came hurrying over.

'I'm sorry, Vlad,' she said. 'I know you're in a hurry but before anyone can get off this plane they have to be sprayed.'

'To be what?' exclaimed Vlad. 'Did I hear right? Did you say sprayed?'

'Yes,' said the hostess patiently. 'Australia is an island, a big island and it is a long way from anywhere else.'

'You're telling me,' interrupted Vlad.

'And,' continued the hostess, ignoring the interruption, 'they want to protect the plants and animals of the country from getting any of the diseases that could be brought in from abroad, so they spray everyone just to make sure there aren't any insects or germs on them.'

'Well, no one is going to spray me,' stated Vlad, 'and that's final.'

'Then you'll have to stay on the plane,' explained the hostess. 'It's the rule: either you get sprayed or you stay on.'

'Not fair,' grumbled the vampire. 'First of all I get

hijacked and then they tell me I've got to get sprayed. Poor old Vlad, poor little Drac.'

The doors opened and men in shorts entered the plane with cans and started to spray around. Vlad flew up to the luggage racks and shouted at them.

'You won't spray me, you knobbly-kneed Australian wombats.'

'What the hell is that?' demanded one of the men, dropping his spray. 'I've never seen anything like it.'

'I'm Vlad the Drac and I'm a vampire,' yelled Vlad, 'and I'm very fierce and dangerous and if you come any nearer I'll vampirise you and your rotten old spray cans.'

'Strewth!' gasped the man.

'If I could have a word,' said Dad, and he whispered in the man's ear.

'He makes a lot of noise but he's harmless, a vegetarian.'

'You don't say,' said the man smiling. 'Right, Terry, Bruce, Kevin.' He called to the other men.

'We've got a vampire here who doesn't want to be sprayed. Come and give us a hand.'

The other three men came and looked at Vlad in amazement.

'Gawd, what is it?' they asked.

'Not it,' said Judy indignantly. 'Him.'

'All right, what's "him"?'

'I'm Vlad the Drac, the famous Vampire from Romania, Great Uncle Ghitza's great-nephew and I'm waiting for you. Come on, spray me, I dare you,' taunted Vlad, baring his fangs.

'You're having us on,' said the first sprayer. 'You're a vegetarian and you're harmless. All right – one, two, three, spray!' And they all pointed their sprays at Vlad and squirted him.

27

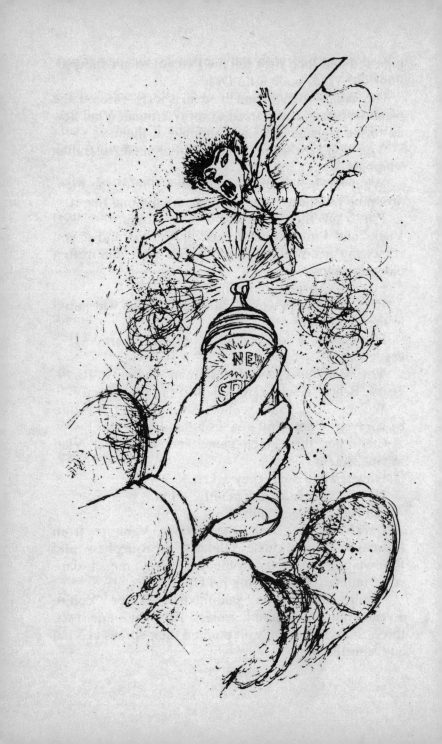

Vlad screeched with indignation as the passengers applauded.

The four men smiled and took a bow and walked off the plane.

'I *knew* I wouldn't like Australia,' moaned Vlad, 'and I don't. On top of everything else I smell of that rotten stuff.'

Judy wiped him with a handkerchief and tried to comfort him.

'Never mind, Vlad, soon you'll be on your way home. This time next week you'll be back with your family, just try and think about that. How nice it will be for you to see Magda and Mum and Dad and Judy and Paul and Ghitza.'

'I don't think I can face it, Judy,' whispered Vlad. 'I'm so tired, I've been flying for days and days and I'm very, very jet lagged and I don't want to go on another plane. I need a rest on dry land for a while.'

Judy was feeling rather dazed herself. It had been a long flight and there was a time difference of ten hours.

'Poor old Vlad,' she said sympathetically. 'I can imagine how you feel; I feel pretty weird and I didn't come from California first. Still, I don't know what we're going to do.'

'You must tell the Lord High that I'm tired and need to rest before I go home.'

'Oh no,' groaned Judy.

'You don't love me either,' sniffed Vlad, close to tears.

'Oh Vlad,' said Judy stroking his head. 'Of course I do, but I don't fancy being the one to tell Dad that you want to spend a bit of time with us before you go home.'

'I honestly do not understand that man,' said the

vampire. 'It's not as though I ever did him any harm. I have never behaved in any way to suggest that I am anything but a model vampire but the Lord High has these funny ideas. Poor old Vlad, poor little Drac.'

The Stones and Vlad were allowed off the plane first as Mum had a baby and they immediately got in the line to go through Passport Control. Vlad sat on Judy's shoulder looking miserable. One of the air hostesses went and had a word with the man checking the passports. He looked up sharply as she whispered in his ear.

'A stowaway vampire!' he said in an amazed tone. 'You're kidding. You've got to be joking'

Vlad sniffed indignantly and flew over and stood in front of the immigration officer.

'So you've never heard of a stowaway vampire, have you? Well, I'm not surprised because neither have I. I am not a stowaway, I was hijacked by this man. You should arrest him, it's all his fault. I never wanted to come to Australia, all I wanted to do was go home to my dear wife and my five lovely children and I had the misfortune to meet this man and his family at London Airport and that was the beginning of my problems.'

'Is that right, sir?' asked the immigration officer.

'No, it certainly is not!' shouted Dad and he explained how Vlad had come to fall asleep in Zoe's cot.

The immigration officer looked confused.

'I can tell that it is going to take a while to sort this lot out,' he said. 'You'd better come to my office and we can talk in there.'

The Stones all sat round exhausted as the immigration officer looked through all the rules to see what he should do with Vlad.

'The problem is,' he told Dad, 'there's nothing in

30

here about vampires. There's lots about people and animals but nothing about vampires. I don't know what to do.'

'I don't see why there's a problem,' said Dad. 'Vlad doesn't want to be in Australia. It was all an accident. He wants to go back to his family for Christmas and so it's quite simple. Just put him on a plane back to Romania.'

'Is that what you want?' asked the immigration officer.

'No,' said Vlad.

'What?' yelled Dad. 'But all you've said since we discovered you is that you wanted to get home as fast as possible and that Australia was the last place in the world you wanted to visit.'

'I know,' said Vlad miserably, 'but I'm so tired and jet lagged, I can't face another flight. If I could be spirited back without having to go on another plane, that is what I would want, but I've been flying for three days and I need a break.'

'How come three days?' asked the immigration officer.

'I was visiting my friend Malcolm Meilberg, you know, the film producer in California,' explained Vlad, 'and I was changing planes in London when I got hijacked.'

'Malcolm Meilberg?' said the immigration officer. '*The* Malcolm Meilberg?'

'That's right,' agreed Vlad languidly. 'He's an old friend of mine.'

'Well,' said the immigration officer, looking impressed, 'we'll have to see what we can do to help you in that case.'

'There's nothing you *can* do,' intervened Dad desperately. 'He doesn't have a visa to visit Australia in his passport. You'll have to put him back on the next plane out.'

'I can't face that,' wept Vlad.

'No worries,' said the immigration officer soothingly.

'No worries!' exploded Vlad, 'No worries for you maybe, but I have nothing but worries. I am on the wrong side of the world, I am not going to be home with my family for Christmas, all my luggage is somewhere between London and Romania, I am absolutely exhausted, my friends want to get rid of me and all you can say is no worries.'

'It's just an expression,' explained the immigration officer.

'Well, I never heard it before,' sniffed Vlad.

'That's because it's strine.'

'It's what?'

'Strine – Australian.'

'But I thought people spoke English in Australia. Oh dear, things are getting worse and worse. I won't even be able to talk to anyone.'

'We do speak English,' the immigration officer assured him, 'but it's our own version: strine. Now, to get back to your problem. As you're not a person but a vampire, there's absolutely nothing in the rule book about what to do with you, so I'd better ring up my boss and get a bit of advice.'

So the immigration officer rang for advice but no one knew what to do about vampires. Eventually the Prime Minister was put on the phone. He asked to speak to Vlad.

'Hello, Mr Prime Minister,' said Vlad politely.

'Welcome to Australia,' said the Prime Minister. 'I saw your film the other day and I really enjoyed it.'

'I'm so glad to hear that,' said Vlad.

'Yes, and of course in your case we are delighted to bend the rules and let you stay in Australia for as long as you like. I've told the officer in charge to put that in your passport. I hope you have a good stay.'

'Thank you very much, Prime Minister, you are most kind. I have always wanted to visit Australia and I am proud to be the first vampire to land on your fair shores. Thank you again and goodbye.' Vlad beamed. 'I can stay as long as I like. That is good news, isn't it? Now all I have to do is clear it with Magda and we can all get on with having a good time.'

As they piled into a taxi to go to the hotel Dad asked Vlad, 'How long are you planning to stay? Just a couple of days to recover? Then you could still be back home in Transylvania before Christmas.'

'Yes,' said Vlad, 'something like that. I would like to be home with the kiddies for Christmas.'

Dad looked much relieved and sat back in the taxi to enjoy looking at Sydney.

'It's so hot,' said Judy, peeling off her sweater. 'I knew it would be, but it's still a surprise.'

'It's fantastic,' said Paul. 'Can we go to the beach tomorrow, Mum?'

'We'll see how we all feel,' said Mum. 'It takes a day or two to get over such a long flight. But I don't see why not.'

When they finally got to the hotel they got out of the taxi and staggered into the foyer. As they came in a bald man leapt up to greet them.

'You are Nicholas Stone, perhaps?'

'Yes,' said Dad.

'I am much delighted to meet you,' said the man,

shaking Dad's hand vigorously. 'I am Sir Tibor Bolonsky, the conductor of the New London Philharmonic Orchestra on this tour.'

'How do you do,' said Dad. 'How nice of you to come and meet us. This is my wife Catherine and my children Judy, Paul and the baby is called Zoe.'

Sir Tibor kissed Mum's hand and Judy's.

'Delighted to meet you charming ladies,' he said gallantly.

'What about me,' said Vlad indignantly, 'don't I get introduced?'

'Oh yes,' said Dad weakly. 'This is our friend Vlad the Drac. He's a Romanian vampire.'

Sir Tibor's face lit up.

'Vlad the Drac – the brilliant pianist? You brought him with you? This is wonderful, simply wonderful! The first time I heard you play, Nicholas, was at the Carnival Hall when Vlad did his brilliant performance, that is why I asked for you on this tour. Vlad, it is an honour and a pleasure to meet you. As you are in Australia is there any chance at all that you might consider playing with my orchestra?'

'Vlad has to get home by Christmas,' Mum intervened hastily. 'His wife and five children are expecting him.'

'Ah, this is a big disappointment for me,' said Sir Tibor wringing his hands. 'I have promised to do some extra performances in Australia to raise money for the endangered species. Now, if Vlad were with us I think we could be raising far more money.'

'You want me to play the piano with an orchestra?' asked Vlad.

'Of course,' said Sir Tibor. 'After your performance in the wonderful film in which I saw you, people will pay a lot of money to hear you.'

'You have to go home, Vlad,' said Judy.

'Yes,' agreed Paul. 'Ghitza and the other children will be so miserable if you aren't there for Christmas.'

'You can't leave Magda to cope all on her own *again*,' said Mum,

'And you never wanted to visit Australia anyway,' Dad reminded him. 'You certainly don't want to spend two months here.'

'It's my duty,' said Vlad. 'If I can raise money for endangered species then I must put personal considerations behind me and sacrifice myself and if necessary my family to the general good. If Sir Tibor thinks thousands of people will pay money to come and listen to my music then I cannot disappoint my public. Sir Tibor, at great personal cost, I agree to perform at as many concerts as you want.'

Sir Tibor beamed.

'Ah, this is wonderful! And your friends will be so happy to have you with them for a longer time. Nicholas, if I can rely on you to look after Vlad for me, I am sure I can offer you a permanent post when we all return to London.'

'I thought Hungarians and Romanians didn't get on,' said Dad glumly.

'You are quite right, but so far from Europe it is nice to meet someone from near my home. Anyway, here we are in a new country, why would we bring old grudges in our baggage? Vlad, welcome to Australia.'

'Thank you,' said Vlad gratefully.

'Anyway, Transylvania was for hundreds of years a part of Hungary – in fact that is where my own family come from.'

'Ah,' said Vlad enthusiastically. 'Maybe it was some of your ancestors that my Great Uncle Ghitza vampirised.'

'Yes,' agreed Sir Tibor. 'That is indeed quite possible.'

'In that case,' Vlad pointed out, 'I may have some of your blood in my veins – I mean we're almost related, blood brothers sort of.'

Vlad and Sir Tibor laughed heartily at the thought. Judy looked round and suddenly realised that they were the only people in the hotel foyer. She tugged at Dad's sleeve.

'Dad, everyone's run away. Vlad isn't as famous in Australia as he was in England.'

'Oh no,' groaned Dad. 'I'm absolutely worn out, I don't know what to do.'

'I think we ought to let as many people know about Vlad's being here as we possibly can,' said Paul, 'or life will be impossible.'

'So what else is new?' muttered Dad. 'But you're right, Paul. Sir Tibor, I will have to put a condition on my agreement to take care of Vlad. We can only take on this onerous burden if you arrange for him to be on radio, on TV and in every possible paper. As you can see people are terrified of him; we'll be totally isolated if the Australian public aren't made aware of his vegetarian convictions.'

Sir Tibor looked around, the only person he could see was hiding behind a pot plant. He roared with laughter.

'Ha, you make them very afraid, Vlad, just like your Great Uncle, eh? Still, I see it can perhaps be a problem. Have no fear, Nick, I have many contacts who will help with this little difficulty. By tomorrow night Vlad will be the most famous vampire in Australia.'

'Will you be well enough, Vlad?' asked Mum. 'I feel exhausted and you've been further than me.'

'Have no fear,' Vlad assured her. 'Exhausted though

I am, the Great Australian Public will not be let down.
I shall be there, Sir Tibor, never fear. Transylvania
expects every vampire to do his duty and I shall not
shirk.'

3

CROCODILE VLAD

By the time Sir Tibor finally drove off, the Stones felt absolutely exhausted. They dragged their luggage into the hotel lobby and Dad went over to the reception clerk to ask for their keys.

'G'day,' said the man at the desk pleasantly.

'Good day!' snapped Vlad, from the safety of Dad's pocket. 'Whatever do you mean, you stupid Aussie turnip head? Good day indeed in the middle of the night. Are you blind or something, or just stupid?'

'Listen, mate,' said the man standing up and staring angrily at Dad. 'I don't need you coming in here and insulting me. I don't have to take this from you. Now you apologise or I'll thump you.'

Dad sighed. 'It wasn't me,' he said wearily. 'It was him.'

'That's right,' cried Vlad belligerently, climbing out of Dad's pocket and standing on his shoulder. 'It was me. Do you want to make something of it? Do you want a fight? Come on then, let's see you put up your bunches of five,' and Vlad jumped up and down on Dad's shoulder with his fists clenched, like a boxer's.

The reception clerk stared in disbelief.

'What is it?' he gasped.

'It's Vlad the Drac,' explained Dad. 'He's a vegetarian vampire and he's staying here with us, I'm afraid.'

'Too scared to fight me, eh?' shouted Vlad. 'Come on, Aussie, put your fists up and show what you're made of. Good day in the middle of the night indeed, you must be barmy.'

'Now calm down, mate,' said the reception clerk. 'Australians say g'day at any time of day or night.'

'That's daft,' complained Vlad. 'How can it be a good day when it's night?'

'Not good day but g'day,' said the clerk. 'It's quite different.'

'Oh,' said Vlad. 'More strine?'

'That's right, mate,' said the receptionist. 'Welcome to Australia, Vlad. I saw yer film. Good movie that.'

'Well, thank you,' said Vlad. 'Maybe I won't fight you after all.'

'Whew, that's a relief,' said the receptionist. 'I'm sure you'd have given me one hell of a beating. You're in rooms 214 and 215, Mr Stone. I'll get someone to bring the bags up for you.'

'Thanks,' said Dad wearily.

'No worries,' replied the receptionist. 'See you later.'

'You will not see us later,' said Vlad indignantly. 'It is now half past eleven: if you see us any later it will be tomorrow and it will be earlier, so why do you keep saying silly things?'

'More strine, Vlad,' explained the receptionist, 'you'll have to get used to it. See you later is the Australian way of saying goodbye, you know, see you around, that sort of thing.'

'It's all very confusing,' moaned Vlad. 'They tell you it's an English-speaking country, but it only sort of is.'

That night all the Stones and Vlad slept heavily.

Dad was woken by the telephone. It was Sir Tibor.

'A million apologies that I wake you so early,' he said, 'but I have arranged for Vlad to be interviewed upon the TV and after that I make a press conference and after that an interview upon the radio. Good?'

'Yes, very good,' mumbled Dad sleepily.

'Nick, you go back to sleep. I'll be in a little while round and take Vlad. Could you ask him please to be down in the hall at about midday? Don't let him keep me waiting.'

'Sure,' said Dad, 'I'll give him the message. He'll be there all right. Nothing he likes as much as a bit of publicity.'

Dad staggered out of bed and gave Vlad the message and then slept through till about eleven o'clock. They all had a late breakfast and then decided to go off and explore Sydney a bit. It was a lovely hot day and they enjoyed just walking along in the sun and looking at the city sights in the daytime.

'Let's walk down to the harbour,' suggested Mum. 'We can look at the bridge and the Opera House.'

On the way they passed a TV shop. One of the televisions in the window was on and a huge crowd had gathered outside. Dad jumped up to catch a glimpse over people's heads.

'It's Vlad all right,' he told the family. 'Sir Tibor has organised it really well.'

Feeling much relieved, they began to enjoy themselves. They were bowled over by the huge harbour and the magnificent bridge that linked the two sides. They took photographs of each other in front of the bridge and then strolled over to the Opera House to have lunch. They sat out in the sun and watched the little sailing boats bobbing up and down on the blue water.

'This is the ticket,' said Dad. 'Whoever said that Sydney has the best situation of any major city was dead right. It's unbelievable! What a view and what a climate. If only Vlad wasn't here with us, we could have a fantastic holiday.'

'We'll have to put up with it, Nick, and try to have a good time anyway,' said Mum. 'Try not to get riled by Vlad. Just think about how good it will be for you to have a secure job when we get back home. It will make such a difference, not only financially but to how you feel about yourself. You're a good violinist, you deserve some recognition.'

'Yes, Dad,' agreed Judy, 'and we are used to Vlad.'

'Speak for yourself,' groaned her father.

'Judy's quite right,' agreed Mum, 'and it isn't for long.'

'What did Sir Tibor mean about extra concerts to raise money for endangered species?' asked Paul. 'I was so tired, I hardly took it in last night.'

'Concerts to raise money for pandas and whales and things, I suppose,' Dad said.

'That's great,' said Paul enthusiastically. 'And if Vlad's being here can help raise money for that, then I'm game to put up with all the trouble we'll run into.'

'I suppose you're all right,' sighed Dad, 'but it is so peaceful without him. It was bad luck being at London Airport at just that minute. Still, I suppose it's better to be here with Vlad, than not at all.'

As they walked back to the hotel they passed several newspaper stalls and saw that there were headlines like 'Vlad's First Bite at the Lucky Country' and 'Vampire Vlad to perform for Endangered Species' and 'Vampire Filmstar's Aussie Trip'.

When they eventually got back to their hotel and turned on the radio, there was Vlad telling the interviewer all about Mrs Vlad and the five children and the Stones, and his Great Uncle Ghitza and Malcolm Meilberg and *Marauding Monsters of the Outer Galaxy*, and how he had always wanted to visit Australia and how helpful the Prime Minister had been and how happy he was to be there.

'He's such an accomplished liar,' commented Paul.

'Maybe he's coming round to the idea of being in Australia,' said Judy. 'I mean, with all the publicity he's getting. It's just what he loves.'

'Don't I know it,' groaned Dad. 'Well, let's hope that you're right. It would make the next couple of months easier for all of us.'

A little later Sir Tibor brought Vlad back.

'The publicity worked very well, I think,' said Sir Tibor. 'We were walking here, Vlad and I, and everyone, but everyone, wanted Vlad's autograph. There will be no more misunderstandings now, Nick.'

'You underrate Vlad,' Dad told him, 'but thanks for all the trouble you've been to.'

'Not at all, it was a grand pleasure,' Sir Tibor assured him. 'One Transylvanian to another, eh, Vlad? Now, I wonder, would you perhaps like to stay in the flat I am renting here? It is very lovely, looking out on the Harbour. Myself, I will be away for Christmas and it will be empty. With a baby, it would be much more comfortable I think than a hotel.'

'That would be wonderful,' said Mum gratefully. 'Hotels are not ideal with young children.'

'It's a wonderful offer,' said Dad nervously, 'but I'm not sure we'll be able to afford the rent.'

'Rent!' shouted Sir Tibor. 'Rent, who said anything about rent? You look after my favourite vampire for me and I'll do you a favour by giving you my flat. Is not fair, yes?'

'Well, thanks,' said Dad. 'I'm most grateful.'

'Excellent, then that's settled. Here's the key and the address. Everywhere I have left notes to say where to find things and here is the number which I am staying at. So if anything is not all right, you ring me there. So why should you hang around here, why not move in this day?'

And so it came about that two hours later the Stones were installed in Sir Tibor's luxury flat. Vlad slept all the way through the move and only woke up an hour or so after they had arrived.

'Where am I?' he asked weakly.

So Judy explained to him all about Sir Tibor and the flat. 'It's got the most super views over the harbour, Vlad, and all mod cons and we don't have to pay for it.'

'Yes,' said Vlad carelessly. 'That's how it is when you take up with a vampire. See all the nice things that happen to you? I hope even the Lord High will be nice to me now.'

'What would you like to do for the rest of the day, Vlad?' Judy asked.

'I want to go to a library,' Vlad told her. 'I need to find out about endangered species if I'm going to give concerts on their behalf. What is an endangered species, Judy?'

'Creatures of which there are very few left and which are in danger of dying out completely.'

'Like vampires!' shrieked Vlad. 'Oh well, then I must get boned up on it. That is something I *really* need to know about. Call me a cab, Judith, and tell the driver I want to go to the central library.'

Judy took Vlad down to the street and hailed a cab and explained about Vlad.

'No worries,' said the driver. 'I'll take him there and bring him back on condition he gives me his autograph for my children, Vlad.'

'With pleasure,' Vlad told him. 'No worries. Now

44

on to the central library.'

When she got back, Dad was in the kitchen singing to himself as he cooked the family some supper.

'Hi,' he said smiling. 'Is Vlad awake yet, Judy? Do you think he'll want to eat with us?'

'No,' Judy told her father. 'He rushed off to the library to catch it before it closed.'

'The where?' exclaimed her father.

'The library,' said Judy again, slowly and loudly.

'That's what I thought you said,' mused Dad, as he turned the meat over. 'What's it all about?'

'He's reading up on endangered species, a kind of preparation for the concerts he's going to perform in. I think he feels that vampires are an endangered species so he's very involved in the problem.'

'Umm,' said Dad, singing even louder. 'Australia is obviously having a good effect on him; maybe he'll spend every spare moment in the library. This is a positive development. All right, everyone! Supper's ready, come and eat. I've set the table out on the balcony, so we can look over the harbour while we eat.'

Just as they finished eating Vlad returned, accompanied by the taxi driver carrying a huge pile of books.

'Put them down over there, please,' Vlad told him, 'then I'll give you my autograph for your children.'

'Gee, thanks, Vlad,' said the taxi driver. 'That will give the kids a real thrill for Christmas. Must be off. Happy Christmas all.'

'Happy Christmas,' they all chorused back.

Dad looked at the pile of books with satisfaction.

'My goodness, Vlad, what a lot of books. You will have to work hard over Christmas. Still, don't worry, we'll be very considerate and go out and leave you to it.'

'Hum,' said Vlad dubiously. 'I did a lot of reading in the library and all work and no play makes Vlad a dull vampire. So tomorrow I would like us all to go to the zoo.'

'On Christmas Eve?' said Paul.

'Why not?' demanded Vlad. 'I mean it's very hot, not like a real Christmas.'

'Yes, why not,' agreed Mum. 'I'd like to get out tomorrow and it's not far. Look at the map here, it's called Toronga Park. It's on the other side of the harbour. It's the least we can do for Vlad, since he's responsible for us having such a wonderful place to stay.' Vlad smiled modestly.

The next day they set off early for the zoo. 'How are we going to get there?' asked Vlad.

'By boat,' Dad told him. 'Look at this map: we're here and there's the zoo, so we go down to Circular Quay here and pick up a ferry to take us to the other side of the harbour.'

'I've never been on a boat,' said Vlad. 'Fancy going on a boat in a big city. Much better than a bus or that rotten old tube train we went on in London.'

They walked down to the waterside where the Ferry Terminal was and Dad bought the tickets to take them over. Vlad sniffed in the sea air.

'It makes me feel very healthy,' he told the Stones as he sat on the edge of the railings.

'I wouldn't sit there if I were you, Vlad,' Mum said. 'Once it starts to move you might get blown off.'

'Leave Vlad alone,' Dad told her. 'If he wants to sit there, let him. Stop telling everyone what to do.'

'I like it here, no worries,' Vlad assured her. 'We vampires are an intrepid lot.'

The ferry started to chug across the harbour, a slight breeze cooled them and they were all enjoying the trip. Suddenly the ferry swerved abruptly to avoid a tug. Vlad swayed and then with a shout landed in the water.

'Vampire overboard!' shouted Paul.

Judy threw out a life belt and craning over the side she saw Vlad struggling to grab hold of it.

'Are there many man-eating sharks in the harbour?' asked Dad hopefully.

'Don't worry, Vlad,' called Paul. 'I'm coming in to get you,' and he kicked off his shoes and dived in. A minute later he surfaced holding Vlad in his right hand. Everyone on board had rushed over to that side of the boat. As Paul was pulled back on board everyone cheered. Vlad bowed and turned to Paul.

'Thank you, Paul,' said Vlad. 'When I get back to Transylvania I shall see to it that you are awarded the Order of the Blood of St Ghitza and are made a Companion of the Vampires of the Cold Bath. These honours are rarely given and are in recognition of services to vampires beyond the call of duty. It will be the first time a human being has been so honoured. Now, let us lie in the sun and dry out before we get to the zoo.'

When they arrived Mum asked Vlad what he wanted to see first.

'The pandas,' he said.

'Why the pandas?' asked Judy.

'You'll see,' Vlad told her as they walked over to the panda enclosure. They had to stand in a queue because so many people had come to see the Chinese visitors. When the Stones finally reached the front Vlad was sitting on the wall, staring at the pandas with a sad look in his eyes.

'Poor little pandas,' he muttered. 'They're so pretty, all cuddly and black and white. You'd think people would be kinder to them. I mean vampires have all kinds of good points but no one could call us pretty.

You know, I really feel for those pandas, being vegetarians and everything.'

Then he yelled at the two pandas who were strolling around and quietly eating bamboo shoots.

'Hey there, you pandas! You don't have to worry. I'm here to speak for you. *I'll* tell the people what it's like to be an endangered species.'

The pandas went on eating their bamboo shoots. Vlad looked hurt.

'They don't understand,' Judy told him.

'Mmmmm,' said the vampire. 'Well, maybe if I get a bit closer and shout they'll get the message.'

'Careful, Vlad!' called Mum, but it was too late. Vlad stood on a bamboo branch shouting at the pandas and talking very slowly.

'I-am-here-to-speak-for-you. Understand?'

The pandas went on munching away at the succulent green bamboo shoots, until one decided that Vlad was a tasty looking green morsel and made a lunge at him.

'Vlad!' yelled Judy and Paul together. 'Watch it, come back!'

Vlad flew back to them in a huff.

'Well, there's gratitude for you,' he moaned. 'As bad as people.'

'They don't mean any harm,' said Mum soothingly. 'They would respond very positively if they understood. They come from China, you see. They're not used to vampires.'

'Where now, Vlad?' asked Dad.

'I want to go and see the crocodiles,' Vlad told him.

'Why crocodiles? They're not an endangered species.'

'Precisely, but they were a while back. I want to ask them how they managed to reverse the trend. I

49

mean crocodiles are Australians, so they'll probably speak English or at least strine.'

'Vlad, I don't think that talking to crocodiles is a good idea,' remonstrated Mum. 'They're very . . .'

'You're so bossy,' interrupted Dad. 'If Vlad wants to go talk to crocodiles on matters of mutual interest who are you to interfere? Come on, Vlad, into my pocket and we'll run over to the crocodiles.'

As Vlad climbed into his pocket, Dad shouted, 'See you later.'

As he sprinted off, Mum and the children stared after him.

'I didn't know Dad could run that fast,' said Paul.

'Come on,' said Mum grimly, grabbing Zoe's push chair, 'follow that man.'

Mum and the children rushed after Dad as fast as they could. When they got to the crocodile marsh, Vlad was standing on a log and shouting at Dad.

'It's a swiz. There isn't a single crocodile here.'

As he spoke the log moved and a malicious eye appeared above the water.

'Vlad!' yelled Judy. 'The crocodile! Get out of the way.'

'Crocodiles, Vlad!' shrieked Paul.

Just then the crocodile opened his huge mouth. Vlad lost his balance and nearly fell into the water. The crocodile was poised to snap his jaws shut and swallow Vlad in one gulp, but Vlad managed to spread his cloak and fly out of reach. The crowd cheered as Vlad flew back to the Stones. Looking rather shaken, but reluctant to miss a photo opportunity, Vlad bowed and blew kisses.

'That crocodile was very unfriendly,' he said. 'So I decided not to honour him with my company after

all. You knew he wouldn't be nice, didn't you?' Vlad accused Dad.

'Yes, that was very bad of you, Nick,' Mum told Dad severely. 'We were really scared.'

'Scared, were you?' said Vlad casually. 'How interesting. I wasn't, not one bit. Oh well, there you are, I'm Crocodile Vlad, the fearless vampire,' and he smiled as he posed for photographs on the edge of the crocodile enclosure.

4

AVOID THE VAMPIRE

'It doesn't feel a bit like Christmas Eve,' commented Paul as they ate their supper on the balcony.

'It most certainly does not,' agreed Vlad. 'Whoever heard of nearly being eaten by a crocodile on Christmas Eve?'

'Can we go down to the beach tomorrow?' asked Paul. 'Just as we planned in London.'

'Umm,' agreed Dad. 'That sounds good. We'll take some turkey sandwiches and have a good time swimming and sunbathing. Sound all right to you, Judy?'

'Great!' said Judy enthusiastically.

'Sunbathing on Christmas Day!' exclaimed Vlad. 'You must be potty.'

'Why?' demanded Paul.

' 'Cos everyone knows that Christmas happens in the middle of winter, so this can't be Christmas.'

'Vlad, this is the southern hemisphere, you know that. So here it's Christmas in the middle of summer.'

A tear ran down Vlad's cheek.

'What's up?' asked Mum.

'It's Christmas and I want to be with my family,' wept Vlad. 'Not upside down on the other side of the world in the middle of summer. Poor old Vlad, poor little Drac.'

'Poor Vlad,' said Mum sympathetically, putting him on her lap. 'But at least the family will have your presents and they'll know that you thought of them.'

53

'But *I* won't get any presents,' moaned Vlad. 'I'm homesick, I want to go home.'

'I'll phone Sir Tibor,' said Dad quickly. 'I'll explain that you changed your mind, that an unexpected crisis occurred and you had to go home.'

'I can't do that,' Vlad told him. 'My public are expecting me.'

'I suppose that's true,' said Dad gloomily.

'We won't be here long,' Judy pointed out. 'So let's have a good time while we're here.'

Vlad dried his eyes.

'I'll try,' he agreed. 'But it's very hot and vampires don't like the heat. We thrive in snow and ice and sleet and hail.'

The next morning Vlad cheered up considerably when he saw that there were five presents for him,

one from each of the Stones, and a stocking. They were all busily pulling the wrapping off presents when the phone rang. Judy answered it.

'It's for Vlad, from Romania. Vlad, quick.'

'Where is he?' asked Paul.

'I'm in here,' came a muffled voice. 'I'm stuck in the foot of Judy's stocking. Get me out.'

So Judy pulled Vlad out and gave him the phone. Vlad listened and then suddenly his face was wreathed in smiles.

'Yes, of course it's Vlad the Dad,' he cooed, 'and how are my five little darlings? My son Dad is being vampirish! Now that is a nice Christmas present. Yes, after hearing that I most certainly *will* have a happy Christmas. You liked your presents, good, wonderful. Yes, I love you too. Take care of your mother, my darlings. Daddy will be home soon. Happy Christmas. Byeeee.'

Vlad blew kisses down the phone and then he beamed at the Stones as he put it down.

'That was a lovely surprise. Who told them my number? I bet it was you, Mum.'

'No, it wasn't,' she assured him. 'I didn't even think of it.'

'Judy then?' questioned the vampire.

She shook her head.

'So it must have been Paul,' concluded Vlad.

'Not me,' Paul assured him.

Vlad looked hard at Dad.

'You?' he said. 'That was nice of you.'

'It was my Christmas present to you and a sort of sorry about the crocodiles,' Dad told him. 'I wouldn't like to spend Christmas away from my family.'

'Well, I appreciate it,' said Vlad. 'Thanks.'

'Think nothing of it,' muttered Dad, looking pleased.

55

'Come on, let's go down to the beach. I've made lots of sandwiches and Mum has bought Vlad a special bottle of car polish, as it's a celebration.'

Vlad grinned.

'You're all being very nice,' he told them. 'You're my second family. Maybe I don't mind being away so much after all.'

By lunch time the Stones and Vlad were sitting on the sand on Bondi Beach. Paul and Judy raced down to the ocean and Vlad sat on Judy's shoulder staring suspiciously at the sea. They stopped at the water's edge and looked at the huge rollers, as they broke and crashed onto the beach, amid clouds of white spray.

'I'm scared,' whimpered Vlad. 'It's much worse than the sea at Brighton. I don't like it, it's rough and horrible. Take me back to Mum and the Snoglet.'

'That's the Pacific Ocean, Vlad,' Dad told him.

'Pacific!' snapped Vlad. 'Peaceful! I've never seen a more angry sea. Hey, look, there are people riding on the ocean – they'll drown! Quick, call the life guard, get the boats out.'

'It's all right, Vlad, they're surfing, riding in on the surf of the waves. People do it for fun.'

'Crazy,' pronounced Vlad. 'All crazy. I told you Australians were all nutters, even worse than other people. Any sane creature would just stay well away from all this horrible surf and they go and jump in voluntarily, and on Christmas Day too. I give up on people, I really do. So if you people want to risk life and limb in that horrible, unpeaceful ocean, you may do so but please return me to Mum before you do.'

So Vlad sat with Mum and criticised the scene around him. More and more families came down to the beach and laid out picnic tables and windshields, chairs and blankets and brightly coloured picnic boxes

56

containing their Christmas lunch. They covered themselves with cream as protection from the sun, put up huge umbrellas and settled down to enjoy Christmas Day on the beach. They began to play games and as it got nearer to midday, Christmas lunches appeared and soon loads of families were sitting around wearing paper hats and pulling crackers. Vlad stared at them disapprovingly.

'Look at them,' he said in a loud voice, 'behaving as if it were a proper Christmas. I mean, it's too hot and too sunny to be Christmas. It's daft, everyone knows Christmas lunch should be eaten indoors with carol singers outside in the snow and a Christmas tree and things. Definitely not out on a beach, half naked.' The family nearest the Stones looked round.

'You're Vlad the Drac, aren't you?' asked one of them.

'I most certainly am,' agreed Vlad.

'Move over, then, and join the party. It's no fun spending Christmas away from home.'

Soon the Stones found themselves sitting round with the family wearing paper hats and sipping champagne.

'What about a paper hat for Vlad?' said someone.

'They'll be too big,' complained Vlad. 'Made for people as usual; no one thinks about vampires.'

'I'll use one of Zoe's nappy pins to make one smaller,' said Mum.

'And here's a clip from my hair to keep it on with,' said Judy.

Complete with red paper hat Vlad began to enjoy himself. Word began to get around that the vampire was on the beach and after a while a small crowd of children gathered round Vlad. Delighted to have an audience, Vlad suggested that all the children play 'Avoid the Vampire'.

'It's not at all difficult,' he assured them. 'You run away and I try to catch you. Anyone who gets caught is vampirised on the spot. All right? I'll count to ten and then you're all for it.'

Soon Vlad was flying round the beach chasing shrieking children who got so excited they ran straight through groups picnicking, upsetting drinks and sending plates flying. People were falling off deckchairs, sun tan lotion was poured into glasses of beer, and general chaos reigned.

'Oh well,' said Judy philosophically, 'it didn't take Vlad long to feel at home.'

'No indeed,' agreed Dad. 'In fact it's not bad going. It took him two hours to create total chaos – he usually manages it in less.'

'Don't worry about it too much, mate,' said the man next to them. 'The kids are having a great time. It'll be a Christmas they'll all remember.'

'I think it's getting a bit out of hand,' said Mum. 'You ought to try and get Vlad, Nick. Go on, Judy and Paul, you go and help.'

As they ran along the beach calling out to Vlad, the famous Bondi Beach life savers ran towards them.

'Are you in charge of that vampire?' asked the leader.

'I wouldn't put it quite like that,' Dad told them, 'but he is staying with us, yes.'

'He's certainly creating a lot of trouble. We'll catch him for you, no worries. Come on, fellas, catch the vampire.'

Seeing all the life savers approaching him, Vlad flew up above their heads and yelled tauntingly, 'You'll never catch me alive!'

The life savers raced around the beach but had no more luck than the Stones in catching Vlad.

Eventually they all collapsed onto the sand sweating and exhausted.

'Think of something to do,' they said to Dad. 'It's out of hand. We wouldn't want to call the police but that's what we'll have to do if this goes on. Not much fun spending Christmas Day in a police cell but he won't leave us much choice.'

'I've got an idea,' said Judy.

'She's very hot on vampire psychology,' said Dad. 'When I listen to her things seldom go wrong. So what's the idea, Judy?'

'I think it's winding down,' she told them. 'The children have had enough and Vlad looks exhausted. If we just walk away and leave them, I think it will stop of its own accord.'

Fortunately Judy turned out to be right. After a while all the children had been caught and vampirised and returned to their parents. Vlad flopped down next to Judy.

'I'm exhausted evading the might of the life savers,' he told her. 'I'm hot and sticky, so I am going to sleep for a bit in the shade.'

'All right,' said Judy. 'I'll wake you up before we go.'

'Thank goodness,' said Dad. 'At least we won't end up in the clink.'

When it was time to pack up, Judy looked round for Vlad. She looked under the buckets and in the baby's cot and under the blanket and in the picnic basket, but no Vlad.

'Has anyone seen Vlad?' she asked. 'He went off to have a sleep in the shade and now he's gone.'

Soon everyone was shaking their towels and blankets and swimsuits and emptying the contents of their picnics and shouting.

'Vlad, Vlad the Drac, where are you?'

Then Paul heard a tiny voice yelling, 'I'm in here!'

'He's in our Esky,' said the woman next to the Stones, and she opened the special picnic box they had to keep food cold. 'That's odd because I just emptied it and checked.'

'Vlad does sometimes hide in the most extraordinary places,' Mum told her. They both peered inside.

'There he is,' said Mum, pointing to the inside of the turkey, where a bit of green leg was sticking out.

'Vlad, whatever did you get into the turkey for?'

'To get some shade of course,' Vlad replied indignantly, 'but there was a funny smell in there and a funny taste.'

'That's my stuffing you're talking about,' said the woman huffily.

'I'm sure it's very good stuffing,' Vlad assured her, 'but not the sort of thing vegetarian vampires like. Still, it sheltered me from the sun. Thank you, madam, for lending me your turkey.'

'Don't mention it,' said the woman, 'glad it was useful.'

*   *   *

The Stones enjoyed the beach so much they went back the next day. Vlad decided that beaches were not for him and complained all the time. As they walked wearily back to the flat, he sat in Zoe's pram and declared loudly, 'I shall never, I repeat never, go down to a beach, any beach, again.'

'But Vlad,' said Judy, 'that's partly what a holiday is about, that's one of the things we've come to Australia to do.'

'Oh well,' sighed the vampire. 'You can all go off and have fun in your peculiar people kind of way and

I'll stay home on my own. You needn't worry about me. I can watch TV and read up on endangered species all day. I don't mind not having anyone to talk to day in and day out.'

'Well, I'm certainly not staying in all day for the rest of our time in Australia, in this lovely weather,' Dad told Vlad firmly.

'Poor old Vlad, poor little Drac,' moaned the vampire.

Mum saw a row brewing.

'Nick, dear, why don't you take the children back to the flat. Vlad can come to the delicatessen with me and help me choose supper. Come on, Vlad.'

'Leave me alone,' snapped Vlad. 'I'm not one bit interested in your rotten supper.'

Mum took no notice and picked Vlad up firmly and put him in her pocket.

'You lot go on home, we won't be long.'

Mum went into the shop with Vlad muttering and complaining. When the others were out of sight, Mum took Vlad out of her pocket and put him on the glass counter.

'You can help me choose,' she told him. 'What shall we have?'

Vlad surveyed the rows of sausages and cheeses and cold meats, pickles, octopus and salads with distaste.

'It all looks disgusting,' he told Mum. 'Speaking for myself, I'd rather starve.'

A large man appeared from the back of the shop.

'What's wrong with my food? Get out of my shop. I only keep the freshest . . .'

His voice fell away as he noticed Vlad and then a smile spread across his face.

'Vlad the Drac – welcome to my shop. You stay there for two minutes. I fetch Mama and my camera.

I must take your photograph in my shop.'

He rushed off and returned a few minutes later with a woman.

'Mama, this is Vlad the Drac. Vlad, this is my wife Maria Stanoupolis.'

'Madam,' said Vlad bowing low, 'to meet you is an honour and a pleasure.'

'The vampire who was on TV,' said Maria Stanoupolis. 'Come, Chris, quick, take a picture of me with the vampire.'

So pictures were taken.

'The vampire is with you?' asked Mr Stanoupolis.

'Yes,' admitted Mum.

'Please,' said Mr Stanoupolis. 'You choose whatever you want, no need to pay. To have the vampire here is an honour.'

'It's a pleasure to be here,' Vlad told him, 'and to get some appreciation for a change.'

While Mum selected a variety of mouthwatering foods, Vlad chatted to Chris and Maria Stanoupolis.

'They're from Greece,' he told Mum excitedly. 'Fancy that, I mean it's not far from Romania.'

'If you could ever spare Vlad,' Maria Stanoupolis told Mum, 'Chris and I would love to have him in the shop: the customers would be so excited.'

Mum breathed a sigh of relief.

'We'll miss him, of course, but we could sacrifice him tomorrow.'

'Wonderful!' said Maria Stanoupolis.

'Perfect,' said Mr Stanoupolis.

'I can't wait,' said Vlad. 'Parting is such sweet sorrow. Until tomorrow, dear friends, au revoir, auf Wiedersehn, arrivederci.'

When they got home Mum put out all the food she had bought.

'Yum,' said Judy, 'what a feast.'

'Salami,' yelled Paul. 'My favourite.'

'A bit extravagant, weren't you?' commented Dad, as he watched package after package being unpacked.

'Didn't cost me a penny,' Mum told him smiling.

'No,' chipped in Vlad, 'and all because of me. The man in the deli recognised me and wanted a photo of me and he gave Mum all the food free just 'cos of me.'

'Oh,' said Dad. 'Well, it's lovely food, so thanks.'

Mum poured Vlad some washing-up liquid and he sipped it.

'See what nice things happen to you just because of me?' he said to Dad. 'A free flat, free food. I am a good thing, I really am. Viva Vlad, Viva Vampires!'

The next day Vlad was left at the shop as planned. The Stones had a good day without him and they all went into the shop to collect him on their way back. Vlad was sitting on the counter of the delicatessen with his legs dangling over the side and chatting to all the customers.

'Go on,' he was saying to a woman, 'spoil yourself, have a bit more. The last lady who bought some had to come back and get some more, it tasted so good. Save yourself the extra trip.'

'I'll get too fat,' said the woman giggling.

'Nonsense, madam, nonsense,' said Vlad reassuringly, 'the minute you came through the door I said to myself, Now there is a fine figure of a woman. Just the sort my Great Uncle Ghitza would have liked.'

'Oh, all right,' said the woman. 'Give me double the amount of sausage and an extra portion of cheese.'

As the woman went out, Vlad caught sight of the Stones.

'Hello,' he said. 'I'm very good at selling. I've talked people into buying a lot of food, haven't I?'

'He's been wonderful,' Mr Stanoupolis told them. 'It's been my best day ever. He's a very good business-man.'

'Business vampire,' Vlad corrected him.

'Could Vlad come tomorrow?' asked Mrs Stanou-polis. 'Or is that too much to ask?'

'No, no,' Dad assured them. 'If he's good for business, we'll find a way of doing without him for another day.'

The next day when they dropped Vlad off there was a notice in the window.

'Spend more than $25 and have your photograph taken with the world famous vampire, Vlad the Drac.'

'That was my idea,' said Vlad proudly. 'Chris and Maria are so nice I want to help them. Of course I hate having my photograph taken but there's nothing I won't do for my friends.'

'Well, I hope it goes well,' said Judy. 'Bye, Vlad.'

That evening they stopped off to collect Vlad as usual. Outside the shop was a long queue. When Dad tried to get in, he was told to get to the end of the line as they were all waiting patiently to have their picture taken with the vampire. Inside was Vlad wrapped in a flannel. When he saw the Stones he shouted, 'Gang-way! Make way for my friends there.'

The Stones stared at Vlad.

'Why are you wearing that flannel?' asked Paul.

'Someone came in from Romania,' said Maria Stanoupolis, 'and Vlad got so excited he fell into the taramasalata, so I had to wash his clothes.'

'Yes,' said Vlad. 'It's been so interesting. There have been people in here from seventeen countries all over the world, but now they're all Australians. Isn't that amazing? Chris got me an atlas and I've been looking up all the different countries. I've had a

wonderful time, even if I did fall in the tarama-whatsit.'

'And I have made Vlad some new clothes,' Mrs Stanoupolis told them. 'More suitable for the Australian summer. Look!'

She held up a pair of shorts, a brightly coloured shirt and a small hat with little corks round it.

'Oh no!' groaned Dad. 'I can't bear it, I'll have to look at Vlad's skinny green legs every day.'

'They are no worse than your knobbly hairy white ones,' retorted Vlad. 'Now let me go and don my new attire and then I can get on with having my picture taken. You go on home, I'll join you when my adoring public let me go.'

'I'll bring him home, don't you worry,' Chris Stanoupolis told them. 'And, please, take any food you want. For friends of Vlad, nothing is too good.

5

UP THE HAWKESBURY

One morning Paul tried to wake Vlad up early.

'Wake up, Vlad,' he shouted, as he shook the little vampire. Vlad just turned over.

'Leave me 'lone,' he muttered and went back to sleep.

Paul shook him again. 'Come on, Vlad, you've got to get up. We're going up the Hawkesbury.'

Vlad eventually sat up and glared at Paul.

'Why can't you leave me alone? I don't ask for much. All I want is to be left to recover from my jet lag and you keep pestering me. Poor old Vlad, poor little Drac.'

'All right,' said Paul. 'You go on sleeping while we go up the Hawkesbury.'

'Up the what?' demanded Vlad. 'Where is it you're planning to run off to without me?'

'Up the Hawkesbury River,' explained Paul. 'It's a river not far from Sydney. Mum says it's supposed to be very beautiful and they still have mail boats and we're going on one.'

'A male boat?' said Vlad, brightening up. 'Just us boys then, you and me and Dad?'

'No, Vlad, it's not that sort of male. It's m-a-i-l, as in post, you know, letters, not m-a-l-e, as in man.'

'Oh,' said Vlad, 'so you're all going, Mum and Judy and the Snoglet as well?'

'That's right and if you do want to come you'd better hurry up. We've got to be at the station in under an hour.'

'The station?' said Vlad looking puzzled. 'I thought we were going on a boat.'

'We are, but we have to catch a train to get to the river.'

'A train!' cried Vlad. 'I've never been on a train. Hang on. Hang about, I am definitely coming.'

The Stones and Vlad arrived at the station just in time. They scrambled onto the train and flopped down and a moment later the train set off.

'This isn't a proper train,' complained Vlad. 'I've been tricked. You got me out of my drawer under false pretences.'

'It is a proper train,' growled Paul.

'Jolly well isn't,' replied Vlad. 'It doesn't go chuffety chuff, chuffety chuff, like a real train. There ought to be lots of smoke and black smuts flying around. That's a real train.'

'You've got a very old-fashioned idea of trains, Vlad,' Dad told him. 'Trains haven't been like that for over twenty years.'

'I saw the first train ever in Transylvania,' Vlad told them. 'My mother took me to see it, when I was very small, on the way to Great Uncle Ghitza's funeral.'

'That must have been at least a hundred years ago,' Judy reminded him.

'Yes,' mused Vlad sadly, 'I suppose it must. I always wanted to go on one of those trains that went chuffety chuff and now I never will. I'll just fly around this train and see what it's like.'

'Come back,' shouted Dad. But it was too late, Vlad had disappeared into the next carriage.

70

'I'd better go and look for him, I suppose,' said Judy. 'I won't be long.'

'Bring him back here,' said Mum, 'straight away, before he gets into trouble.'

'I'll try,' said Judy and ran off in the direction Vlad had taken. She walked through the next carriage, but there was no sign of Vlad.

'Excuse me,' she said politely to a woman, 'I know this sounds like a silly question, but has anyone seen my vampire?'

'What are you playing at, young lady?' said the woman indignantly. 'It's not April Fools Day.'

'I know,' said Judy, 'but you see, we're looking after Vlad the Drac and he flew off in this direction.'

'Oh, the tiny vampire who was on the television? Yes, something did fly through the carriage a moment ago. I thought it must be a big moth or something. It went up there.'

The woman pointed at the luggage rack. Judy kicked her shoes off and stood on the seat and looked for signs of Vlad.

'He's not up here now . . .' she began, when she noticed a pair of feet sticking out from someone's luggage. She caught hold of the feet and pulled Vlad out.

'I've got him,' she told the woman, as she climbed down. 'Thanks for your help.'

'What were you doing up there, sticky beaking through my luggage?'

Vlad stood on Judy's shoulder and pulled himself up to his full height.

'Madam,' he declared, 'how dare you accuse me of sticky beaking! Vampires do not sticky beak. You've got some nerve. I've a good mind to vampirise you on the spot.'

'If you weren't sticky beaking, what *were* you doing in my bag?'

'Just looking around,' replied Vlad carelessly.

'If that's not sticky beaking, I don't know what is.'

'What is sticky beaking anyway?' asked Vlad.

'Putting your nose into things that are none of your business.'

'Oh!' said Vlad. 'You mean nosy parkering, minding everyone else's business?'

'Exactly,' said the woman.

'Oh, I'm a sticky beaker all right,' agreed Vlad. 'I'd be a fool not to be. I mean, it's the best free entertainment in town. Oh yes, that's me all right. Vlad the Drac, the champion sticky beaker. Ha, I like learning strine. It's fun.'

The woman laughed. 'Funny little chap, isn't he? Is he always like this?'

' 'Fraid so,' said Judy. 'Thanks for being so understanding.'

'Are you going up the Awkesbury?' asked Vlad. 'We are.'

'It's not Awkesbury,' said Judy sharply. 'It's Hawkesbury.'

'I prefer Awkesbury,' Vlad informed her.

'See you on the boat, Vlad,' said the woman, 'and no more sticky beaking, all right?'

'People always want to spoil my fun,' moaned Vlad, as Judy carried him back to the family. 'Poor old Vlad, poor little Drac.'

Shortly afterwards Vlad and the Stones were sitting on the little steamer and sailing up the Hawkesbury. Dad and Judy were taking photographs.

'Isn't it super, Dad?' said Judy enthusiastically, enjoying the slight breeze in her hair.

'I don't know what you're so enthusiastic about,'

complained Vlad. 'I mean, it's just a river and lots of trees. It reminds me of Romania.'

'It's not one bit like Romania,' snapped Dad. 'Whatever are you talking about?'

'Lots of trees and not many people,' explained Vlad.

Just then the boat began to make for the shore.

'What's going on?' demanded Vlad.

'The boat is delivering mail and all the other things that the people living in the little settlements along the river need,' Mum told him. 'They can't be reached by road, so everything has to come by the river.'

Vlad hung over the side and watched as the mailbag was handed to shore and the boxes of food and other provisions were passed over.

'Ahoy there!' yelled Vlad to the people on land. 'And how are you landlubbers this bright morning?'

'It's Vlad the Drac,' shouted someone. 'Remember that little vampire we saw on television?'

Soon all the other tourists on the boat were asking for Vlad's autograph and getting him to sit on their shoulders and heads for photographs. Vlad began to have a good time. However once everyone had taken a picture they lost interest in him and Vlad began to get tired of the trees and the water. He yawned loudly.

'I'm bored,' he told Judy. 'I don't know about you but I've had enough of the Awkesbury. I think I'll try and get a bit of sleep. Wake me up when we arrive.'

'I will,' she promised and went on looking at the scenery and playing with Zoe.

As they pushed off from another small place, Judy looked around for Vlad. He was nowhere to be seen. Dad sighed and wearily went to find the captain and tell him that Vlad had disappeared. The captain announced over the radio that Vlad was lost and everyone looked in their bags and in their pockets, but there was no sign of Vlad.

'He must have climbed into one of the mail bags,' said the captain. 'I expect we just put him ashore at the last halt.'

'What happens to the mail?' asked Dad. 'Is it just left in the bag or is it delivered?'

'Neither,' said the captain. 'You see, mate, these are very small communities, so whoever collects the bag will put the post into post boxes down by the river and then people come and fetch their mail when they want it.'

'Oh no,' groaned Dad. 'I can't stand it. Look, could you go back and let us check?'

'Sorry, mate,' said the captain. 'I'd like to help but I've got to keep to my schedule. But don't worry; we stop there on the way back. I'll put you off and you can make enquiries about him.'

So when they got back to the jetty Dad and Judy got off. Paul agreed to stay with Mum and Zoe.

'No point in us all going on a wild goose chase,' Dad told her.

'How will you get back down the river, once you've found Vlad?' asked Mum.

'You can ring for a river taxi,' the captain told her. 'It'll cost you an arm and a leg, but you can get them.'

'Wait for us at the launching point,' Dad told her. 'Hopefully we won't be too long and Vlad can pay for the river taxi.'

'See you later,' called Mum and Paul and the other passengers as the boat steamed off, leaving Dad and Judy waving on the jetty.

'I hope we're at the right place, Dad,' said Judy. 'If Vlad got off earlier than we thought he might be further down the river and in trouble.'

'I know,' sighed her father, looking around. 'Well, if Vlad did come in the mail bag, presumably he was posted into one of these post boxes and providing no one has been to fetch their mail yet, he'll still be there.'

So Dad and Judy began banging on the boxes and calling out, 'Vlad, Vlad, are you there? Wake up.'

Dad tried to look in the boxes and shook some to see if they were open. A woman came running down towards them.

'Now you stop that,' she shouted. 'Of all the mean tricks, to try and steal people's mail.'

'Madam,' said Dad patiently, 'I assure you I am not trying to steal anyone's mail, I am merely looking for my vampire.'

'Are you drunk?' demanded the woman backing away. 'Or are you just crazy?'

'We really are looking for a vampire,' insisted Judy. 'His name's Vlad the Drac. Didn't you see him on television?'

The woman looked at them suspiciously.

'I don't have a television,' she told them. 'It was to get away from that kind of thing that I moved to such a remote spot and I don't believe a word either of you are saying. You ought to be ashamed,' she told Dad, 'encouraging the child to tell lies, as well as making them up yourself. I shall call the police and it's no use you trying to get away. There's no way out except by river and the boat's just gone. If you try and steal one of our boats the police will get you in no time. So you just wait there and don't try anything.'

Dejectedly Judy and Dad waited for the police. Soon they saw a small speed boat hurrying towards them. It moored and a big policeman got out.

'That's the man,' the woman told the policeman.

'So what do you think you're doing then, trying to open other people's mail boxes?'

'Now look, officer,' said Dad patiently, 'I know this is hard to believe but we really are looking for our vampire.'

'Don't give me that!' shouted the policeman. 'If you come the raw prawn with me, I'll arrest you on the spot.'

'Look,' said Dad, 'I don't mean to be rude or uncooperative but I don't understand what you're talking about.'

'Coming the raw prawn, pulling my leg, having me on. Now come on, what the hell is going on round here?'

'We look after a little vampire,' Judy told him. 'He's a vegetarian and he's very small and he went to sleep in the mailbag and we think someone may have posted him here by accident.'

'Pull the other one, young lady,' sneered the policeman. 'It's got bells on it.'

'It's true,' Judy told him hopelessly. 'I know it sounds crazy but it was all in the papers and on television. Didn't you see it?'

'I'm a hard-working man,' replied the policeman. 'I don't get much time to watch TV or read and I think you're having me on.'

Just then the buzzer on his walkie talkie went and he picked it up.

'What?' he shouted down the speaker. 'Someone shouting "Let me out", in a postbox downriver! You're right there, mate, it does sound odd, mighty odd. All right, I'll get over there right away.' He put away the walkie talkie and turned to Dad and Judy.

'Right, you two, into the boat,' he said roughly. 'I don't understand any of this.'

So the three of them sped down the river to the next jetty. There was a group of people all standing round the post office staring at a postbox from which came sounds of kicking and shouts of, 'Let me out! I'm suffocating. Open up this minute or I'll vampirise everyone.'

As Dad and Judy and the policeman stepped on shore the local community looked at them.

'Am I ever glad to see you, mate,' said one man to the policeman. 'Twenty years of living on the river and I never heard anything like it. Can't make it out at all.'

'I think this fellow here might be able to shed some light on it,' said the policeman. They all turned and looked hostilely at Dad.

'It's all right, Vlad, we're here,' called Judy. 'We'll have you out in a minute.'

'Judith,' came Vlad's voice, 'a minute is too long. Get me out of here *now*.'

'Will someone please tell me what the hell is going on?' demanded the man.

Dad sighed. 'Well, you see,' he said, 'it's like this. Due to an unfortunate train of accidents, I am looking after a diminutive vampire called Vlad the Drac and . . .'

'I'm not diminutive,' yelled Vlad, 'and I want to be let out.'

'And,' continued Dad in a resigned tone, 'Vlad does silly things and he got into a mail bag on the boat and fell asleep and seems to have been posted and is currently sitting in that box there sounding even more bad tempered than usual.'

'I am not bad tempered,' shouted Vlad. 'I just don't like being posted and it's hot and smelly in here and I want to get out.'

'This vampire, is he dangerous?' demanded the policeman.

'Oh no,' Judy assured him. 'He's a vegetarian. He talks a lot but he's never harmed anyone.'

'That's not true,' interrupted Dad indignantly. 'He's harmed me, I've nearly been arrested. I've nearly been thumped. I'm exhausted and worn out and he's ruining my holiday, but other than that he's harmless. He doesn't suck blood but I would recommend people to have as little to do with him as possible if they want to enjoy life and stay sane.'

'Let me out,' shrieked Vlad, kicking the box and banging with his fists.

'Sounds fishy to me,' said the man in charge of the jetty. 'I don't like the sound of him one bit. If it really is a vampire in there, we've only got your word for it that he's not a bloodsucker.'

'That's right,' agreed the woman. 'I think we should take precautions. Bruce, you go and get some garlic. Betty, you go and get that cross down from the wall of your bedroom, and Fred, you have a bucket of water ready – that's the other thing vampires don't like.'

'Right,' said Bruce. 'And I'll go and get my shot gun just in case it comes in handy.'

'Let me out,' yelled Vlad loudly. 'Let me out this minute, or I'll vampirise the lot of you. Count Dracula will seem like a joke compared to me.'

'Harmless my eye!' commented the policeman sourly. 'Did you hear all those threats he was making?'

'He doesn't mean them,' said Judy. 'He just likes to sound tough; he really is quite harmless.'

'Well, we're not taking any chances,' said Bruce. And they stood round the box, Bruce with his gun pointed at it, Betty clutching her cross, the others clasping bunches of garlic, and one with a bucket full of water ready to drench Vlad if necessary.

'Right. We're ready to go,' said the policeman turning to Dad. 'Here, you take the keys and let the monster out.'

All eyes were on Dad as he opened the post box. There stood Vlad.

'G'day, cobbers,' he said brightly. 'Beaut day, isn't it?'

Just then the bucket of water landed on Vlad, soaking both him and Dad. Vlad yelled in amazement and then looked round at the assembled crowd.

'What's going on?' he demanded from Judy.

'They're scared you might get vampirish,' she told him. 'No one here saw you on television or read about you in the paper, so they're worried.'

'Don't you try anything,' said Bruce, 'or I'll blast your head off.'

'Vampire, I challenge you to look upon this cross,' declared Betty.

'You try anything and it's garlic for you, mate,' said someone else.

'Hah!' shrieked Vlad. 'They're scared of me, just like they would be of Great Uncle Ghitza. But if any of you knew anything about vampires you'd know that they can't stand the light. Now, it is a very hot and sunny day and am I disappearing or fading away? No, I am not, so stop being silly and somebody give me something to eat.'

Just then the policeman's walkie talkie bleeped. Everyone listened as he spoke into it.

'Yes, sarge, we've found him. Yeah, he had been posted just like they said. Yes, well, come on, sarge, it did sound like a bit of a tall story – I mean, a tiddly vegetarian vampire. It doesn't happen every day, you know. I thought they were coming the raw prawn with me. Yeah, sarge, I do read the papers, but it's been a very hard week, Christmas and all, so I missed it. Okay, sarge, I'll sort it out and bring them straight back.'

The policeman glared at Vlad.

'Well, the sarge knew all about you and he wants me to bring all of you back downriver so he can have a picture taken with you. Your wife went and reported what happened,' he told Dad, 'and she's waiting for you with the sarge.'

'So it is true then?' asked the woman with the cross anxiously. 'He really is a vegetarian?'

'So it would seem, lady,' said the policeman.

'Now that everyone feels easier,' said Dad, 'could someone lend me a towel so that I can get dried off.'

'Come back to my place, mate, and have a shower,' said Bruce. 'Nothing ever happens here, this is a special kind of a day. Come on back to my place, everyone, and we'll have a bite to eat before these good folk go on their way.'

So Vlad and Dad and Judy were soon sitting round on the verandah of Bruce's pretty house and eating cake and drinking tea. Vlad was given a special tube of red shoe polish and he had a good time pretending to vampirise them all and had his picture taken with the whole group, red polish all over his teeth and nails.

Betty looked hard at Dad.

'I'm from England, you know,' she told him. 'Came out from Dorset just after the War. In my day no one kept pet vampires in England. Dogs and cats and canaries and budgerigars, but never vampires. Still, people tell me everything has changed.'

'I do assure you,' said Dad, 'it isn't normal even now, and we only do it now and again when Vlad is away from home and that is more than enough.'

'I still get homesick from time to time,' Betty told them. 'I love it here but I still miss my rellies.'

'Really?' said Vlad in a surprised tone. 'I wouldn't have thought you'd have much use for them here. I mean it's so hot and dry.'

'What's the climate got to do with it?' asked Betty, looking puzzled.

'I'd have thought it would be obvious,' said Vlad. 'Why would you need your wellies in the hot weather? You only need them when it's wet.'

81

Betty laughed. 'No, Vlad, not my wellies, my rellies, you know, relations.'

'Oh,' said Vlad. 'I see what you mean, like Great Uncle Ghitza. Yes, I can understand that. I still miss him. Rellies, umm, is that strine?'

'Yes, I suppose it is,' Betty told him. 'You stop thinking about that after a while.'

'I'd better take you people back downriver now,' said the policeman. 'Thanks for the tea, I've really enjoyed it. Makes a change from the usual routine.'

'We've enjoyed it too,' said Dad. 'It's so nice to meet people when you travel and not just see places.'

'There you are,' said Vlad brightly. 'See how much better things are with a vampire around? If it hadn't been for me none of you would have met. I'm a great asset, I really am.'

Dad looked unconvinced. Judy could feel an argument brewing.

'If Mum's waiting with Zoe, don't you think we'd better go quickly?' she suggested.

The whole population of Jacob's Landing gathered at the waterside to wave goodbye to Dad, Judy, Vlad and the policeman. 'Come back any time you want. Stay as long as you like. You're always welcome.'

'Bye, see you later,' yelled Vlad enthusiastically, as the police launch sped away downstream.

6

THE ROAD NORTH

'What I want to know,' said Vlad in an aggrieved tone, 'is why I have to be cooped up in this rotten old car on such a hot day?'

'We're going to the Great Barrier Reef,' Mum told him. 'Sir Tibor needs his flat back and we have three weeks before Dad's first concert, so we're going on a trip.'

'It's too hot,' moaned Vlad. 'And what is the Barrier Reef anyway?'

'It's one of the world's great natural wonders,' Paul explained. 'Look at this map. See, all along the coast of Queensland is this amazing coral reef, with corals made up of wonderful colours and all round the reef are the most beautiful and colourful fishes.'

'Do you mean to tell me that we're stuck in this moving Turkish bath just to look at a whole lot of boring fish?' demanded Vlad.

'No, not just for that,' snapped Dad. 'We want to see something of Australia, explore a bit and have a holiday *and* see the Barrier Reef.'

'It's too hot for that,' complained Vlad. 'I want to be back in the mountains with all the snow.'

'We'll stop a lot on the way,' Judy comforted him, 'and have picnics and take swims.'

'I don't want to go in that horrible rough ocean again,' Vlad grumbled. 'I want to go skating and skiing, not lie around in the boiling sun.'

'This is going to be a *great* holiday,' groaned Dad, as

they sped up the Pacific Highway towards Queensland. As it got near lunchtime they began to look out for somewhere to stop. After a while they passed a waterchute.

'Let's stop here, Nick,' suggested Mum. 'We can have our lunch and the children can cool off in the waterchute. Maybe Vlad would enjoy that as well.'

'Good idea, Mum,' said Judy.

They parked the car and while Mum and Dad organised lunch, Judy and Paul put on their swimming gear and went over to the steps to queue up to go down the chute. Vlad decided to sit on Judy's head and find out just what went on at a waterchute. He looked at the children shrieking as they went round and round the water slide until they eventually landed, splash, in the water at the bottom.

'Why are we waiting?' he asked.

'There's a queue. We have to take our turn,' Judy told him. 'We can't just barge in.'

'I don't see why not,' Vlad replied. 'I'll just threaten to vampirise anyone who gets in our way.'

'Don't you dare,' said Paul severely.

'I don't like all this hanging around. Poor old Vlad, poor little Drac.'

Vlad noticed that some children had started a game of football near the waterchute.

'I can't be bothered with the boring old waterchute,' Vlad told them. 'I'm off to referee that football match.'

And he flew over to the football players.

'Hello, kiddies,' he cried. 'I'm here to referee your football match. I'm Vlad the Drac, the well known vampire referee.'

'I saw you on television,' said one of the children. 'Hey, the vampire who was on TV wants to ref our game.'

'Great! Give him the whistle,' said another child.

Vlad flew up and down, following the game and awarding penalties and laying down the law. At one point two boys were quarrelling over the ball and Vlad flew over and sank his teeth into the football. They all watched with horror as the ball slowly deflated.

'That's your punishment for not playing properly,' Vlad told them. 'I have vampirised your ball and I shall do the same to you if any of you complain.'

Looking very fed up, the children returned to their parents.

'We had to stop playing,' they said. 'The ref vampirised our ball.'

Vlad flew over to Judy and Paul who were still standing in the waterchute queue. Eventually it was their turn.

'Are you coming, Vlad?' asked Judy as she sat preparing to go down.

'I have not been standing in that horrible queue in the sun for my health,' he told her. 'Come on, here we go.'

Vlad squealed with delight as they sped round and round the spiral of the chute, and shrieked as they landed in the water.

'That was great,' he yelled. 'Let's do it again.'

'Lunch first,' said Judy, 'then we'll get in the queue again.'

'Waiting's boring,' complained Vlad.

'You don't have any choice,' Paul snapped.

'That's what you think,' replied Vlad sniffily.

During lunch Vlad disappeared.

'I expect he's gone to sleep,' said Mum. 'You children go and play on the chute for a bit.'

As Judy and Paul ran towards the chute they saw a crowd gathered and heard the sounds of children

crying. Their hearts sank. As they got nearer they saw Vlad standing on the steps shouting, 'All right, kiddiwinks, this is your unlucky day. It's Vampires Only Day on the chute.'

And he put a notice at the bottom of the steps:

> *Vampires Only.*
> *Trespassers will be vampirised on the spot.*
> *signed, Vlad the Drac.*

As the children ran crying to their parents, Vlad had go after go, shrieking with joy as he sped down the slide. A crowd of angry parents gathered round the foot of the chute.

'Who's in charge of this vampire?' demanded someone.

'Yes, who's responsible for him? He's ruining the kids' day,' agreed someone else.

'Can't someone get him down?'

'The first person who sets foot on my chute gets vampirised,' yelled Vlad belligerently.

'Vlad, come here,' called Judy. 'You're not being fair. This is a public chute.'

'Not today it isn't,' Vlad yelled back. 'It's Vampires Only Day today. This is the first Vampires Only Day since the chute opened, so if this isn't fair, I don't know what is.'

'You know this vampire, do you?' asked an enraged parent.

'Well, yes,' said Judy.

'Where are your parents?' demanded a big man. 'I've got something to say to them.'

Dad joined the crowd. 'He's with me,' confessed Dad miserably.

'Well, mate, you'd better do something quickly.'

'Yeah, my kids are hot and miserable. We came here for a quiet day out; we don't need all this hassle.'

'Vlad, come on down this minute,' shouted Dad.

'Won't,' Vlad called back, 'and you can't make me.'

'He's quite harmless, and he's a vegetarian,' Dad told the hostile crowd miserably. 'It's all bluff, you should just ignore him.'

'He's scared the kids,' said one mother. 'It's all very well you saying he's a vegetarian but the children are good and scared.'

'Yeah,' agreed another parent. 'We can't take the risk that he's harmless. He might change into a real vampire for some reason.'

'Vlad,' called Judy.

'I'm not coming down, no matter what you say,' he told her.

'I know,' she shouted back, 'and that's fine. You spend all day on the chute if you like.'

'Traitor,' muttered Dad.

'Some nerve,' grumbled the crowd.

'I just thought,' continued Judy, 'that you might get thirsty and I've got a nice cold bottle of washing-up liquid here. Would you like some?'

'Now that's very thoughtful of you, Judy. You always were the only one who understood me. All right, bring it to me up here.'

'I'll bring it in the Esky, then you can have some when you want it and it will stay cold.'

'Good idea,' said Vlad. 'You can come up if you want to.'

Judy walked up the steps with the crowd watching and mumbling disapproval. When she got to the top she opened the Esky. Vlad stuck his head in to investigate the contents. Judy pushed him in and snapped the lid shut. Then she held the Esky up in the air for the crowd to see. They cheered and cheered as she came down the slide, holding the Esky above her head.

'Well done, Judy,' said Dad.

'That was fast thinking,' commented Paul.

'Judas Judy,' came a muffled voice from inside the Esky.

'You need to keep that vampire on a tighter rein, mate,' said one father. 'He really upset the kids.'

'Yeah,' agreed another. 'You should have known better than to bring him here. First he vampirises the ball and ruins the kids' football match. They cost money, you know. And then, as if that wasn't enough, he goes and monopolises the chute. You don't get a moment's peace with that vampire around.'

'We're going,' said Mum quickly. 'Don't worry, we'll take him away, right away. Come on, Nick, come on, children.'

'Get a birdcage for him,' someone called after them. 'That should keep him out of mischief.'

The Stones scrambled into the car and drove away from the angry crowd.

'Leave Vlad in the Esky to cool off,' said Dad grimly. 'You did very well, Judy, and I feel like a nice peaceful drive, while I think about that birdcage suggestion.'

Towards evening Dad relented and Vlad was allowed out.

'I'm soaking wet,' he complained. 'And you shut me up in that cold box.'

'Poor old Vlad, poor little Drac,' they chorused.

'Quite so,' agreed the vampire. 'Where are we going now?'

'We're looking for a motel to stay in for the night,' Judy told him.

'Oh, Judas Judith,' said Vlad spitefully. 'You are

89

ignorant, as well as not being my friend. It is not mo-tel but ho-tel, heh as in happiness, hospital, horse, hail, hopeful, handkerchief, Hungary, Hobart, hen, haddock, hazelnut, Hamlet, hedgehog, hyacinth, Harry, Helena, hamburger and 'Awkesbury. *Ho*-tel. Do you get it?'

'Well, actually, Vlad, it is *mo*-tel. It's a hotel where you take your car.'

'If you think,' declared Vlad, 'that I'm going to sit down to breakfast with a car for company you are much mistaken.'

Eventually they found a motel, booked two rooms and then went out to look for somewhere to eat. They found a Vietnamese restaurant and went in. The man standing behind the counter greeted them cheerfully.

'G'day. I'm Mr U-Loc. You want to eat from the menu or have a smorgasbord Vietnamese style?'

'What's that?' asked Dad.

'Oh, you pay $10 each, and you take a plate and take as much food as you want. It's all laid out here, you see.'

'It looks super,' said Judy.

'Smells lovely,' sniffed Mum.

'Yummy,' agreed Paul.

'Right, smorgasbord for four,' said Dad.

'And what about me?' demanded Vlad, standing on the counter looking indignant.

Mr U-Loc's face lit up.

'It's Vlad the Drac,' he said. 'Oh, welcome to my restaurant. I saw you on TV.'

'Ah,' said Vlad. 'That's nice. But though your food looks quite excellent it isn't the kind of thing I eat.'

'You wait there,' said Mr U-Loc. 'For you, Vlad, I make a special smorgasbord.' He disappeared into the kitchen and Vlad waited patiently while the Stones eagerly piled their plates high with fried rice, sweet and sour pork, chilli beef, spring rolls and a vast choice of other delicacies. Soon Mr U-Loc returned with a tin of floor polish, a bottle of window cleaner, a bar of soap, a huge box of water softener and a packet of scouring powder all decorated with Vietnamese mint and coriander.

'There, Vlad,' he said proudly, handing him a plate. 'You take what you like – a special smorgasbord for you – no one else will be allowed to touch it.'

'Thank you very, very much,' said Vlad, looking delighted and licking his lips. 'That is most thoughtful of you.' Vlad helped himself to a big helping of every-thing.

'You want to eat with a spoon or chopsticks?' asked Mr U-Loc.

'I'll try chopsticks like the others,' said Vlad.

They all sat round tucking into their supper, enjoying every mouthful, although Vlad did have a problem with the chopsticks.

'I'm not getting any food,' he moaned. 'How do you use these silly things?'

'May I join you?' asked Mr U-Loc.

'Please do,' said Mum and Dad.

'I show Vlad how to use the chopsticks,' said the restaurant owner, and he stood behind Vlad and guided him until the vampire had got the idea.

'Look at me,' cried Vlad, once he had grasped it. 'I'll race you all. I bet I finish first.'

'Mr Vlad, could I perhaps take a photo of you please?' asked Mr U-Loc. 'It will be very good for my business.'

'Certainly,' said Vlad. 'I understand about these things. I'm a business vampire myself. Now let me write an appreciation on the menu.

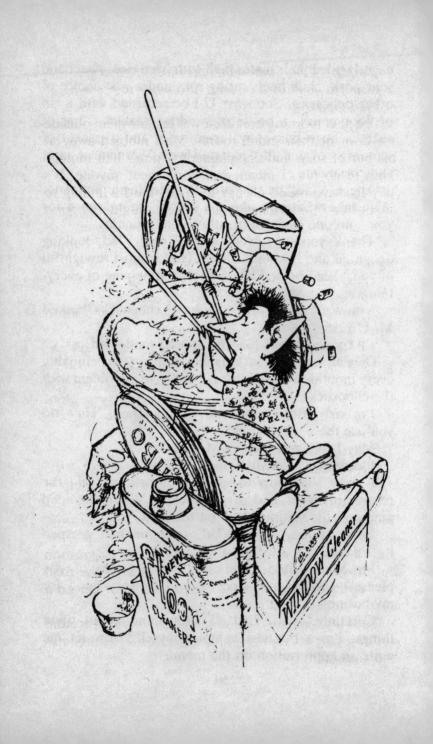

'To Mr U-Loc, who makes the most original smorgasbord in Australia (and probably the world). Vlad the Drac.'

The next morning breakfast was left for them outside the door of their motel rooms. Vlad nibbled away at his bar of soap and complained: 'I don't like motels. They're no fun. I mean, you don't meet anyone. It's silly to drive round all day in a car, hardly talking to anyone and then you stay in a motel at night and don't meet anyone, so you might as well stay at home.'

'I hate to admit it,' said Dad ruefully, 'but I think Vlad's right. Tomorrow night we'll stay in a hotel.'

The next day they drove for about eight hours. As it began to get dark, Dad took over the wheel from Mum.

'We should stop soon,' said Mum. 'We're all exhausted.'

As they drove through sections of the road with bush on either side, Vlad noticed that there were signs by the road, with pictures of kangaroos and wombats on them.

'What do they mean?' he asked.

'That there are likely to be animals crossing the road and not to go too fast. Then you can stop if a kangaroo or wombat strays on to the road.'

'Drive very carefully!' Vlad told Dad. 'Slowly, slowly, be very careful of the animals.'

Dad was slumping across the wheel with exhaustion but drove with great caution. At the side of the road they noticed a dead kangaroo and a little further on a dead wombat. Vlad got very upset.

'Poor little animals,' he sniffed. 'Just hopping around and enjoying life and some rotten person in a car comes and runs them over.'

93

'They didn't do it on purpose,' Judy told him. 'The animals don't understand about traffic and just jump out on to the road.'

'That's all well and good, Judith,' Vlad told her. 'But who owns the cars and who builds the roads? I don't know about you but I never saw a wombat drive a car yet or indeed a kangaroo. It says in all the books I read that those animals come out at dusk, so I think we should stop at the next town to help protect the poor little animals.'

So they stopped at a modest hotel in the main street of a small town. They all had a shower to freshen up after the day's drive and then ran downstairs for supper. They sat at a big table in the middle of the dining room and Zoe slept peacefully in her cot. Vlad looked round and sniffed disapprovingly.

'This isn't like other hotels I've stayed in. It's not like the Ritz in London. It's small and it's very hot and the carpet is worn out and the wallpaper, well, it's awful. Who'd want to stay here? Can't we go somewhere else?'

'Vlad, be quiet,' said Mum, blushing with embarrassment.

'Are we going to get served or aren't we?' continued the vampire loudly.

'Shut up!' snapped Dad. 'You'll get us all thrown out.'

'I'd be doing you a favour,' Vlad assured him. 'I shall go and ring the bell for service.' And he flew over and began to ring the bell loudly and persistently, calling out, 'Coo-ee, anybody there?'

A waitress ran in.

'G'day,' she said pleasantly. 'Are you ready to order?'

'Ready?' said Vlad. 'I should say we are ready

and have been for the last hour.'

'Take no notice of him,' said Dad shuffling around uneasily. 'He enjoys being rude. Now, I would like steak and salad. What will you have, children?'

'Hamburger and chips, please,' said Paul.

'Me too, please,' said Judy.

'And I'll have a mushroom omelette and salad, please,' said Mum.

'One steak, two hamburgers, one mushroom omelette. And what about your little friend here?'

'There is nothing on this menu,' announced Vlad, 'that I would be caught dead eating – in fact, I probably would be dead if I ate it.'

The waitress looked at Vlad with amusement.

'He's quite a character, isn't he?' she said, smiling. 'A real Pommie Whinger.'

'Pommie Whinger?' exclaimed Vlad. 'What's she on about?'

'A whinger is someone who is always moaning,' Mum told him.

'Oh,' said Vlad brightening up, 'poor old Vlad, poor little Drac and all that? Complaining and carrying on? Oh yes, I'm a whinger all right. Good fun whinging. It's my favourite hobby. Listen to this, poor old Vlad, hijacked to Australia, separated from his family, spends Christmas all alone, locked up in an Esky. No one is as badly treated as me. Vampires are persecuted by people and it's not right. Poor old Vlad, poor little Drac. Now was that or was that not a champion whinge?'

'It certainly was,' said the waitress laughing. 'Good on yer, Vlad.'

'And what's a Pommie?'

'Someone from England.'

'But I'm not from England,' said Vlad outraged.

'How could you think such a thing? I'm a Transylvanian vampire from Romania. Pommie indeed!'

'Maybe you're a Rommie Whinger?' suggested Judy.

'Yes,' said Vlad sounding pleased, 'that's what I am. Vlad the Drac, the Champion Rommie Whinger. Now, young lady, don't just stand there. Go and get these four pommies their suppers before they start whinging – you know what they're like.'

7

ON THE REEF

'How long are we going to spend on this rotten island?' demanded Vlad. 'I don't like being surrounded by the sea. I'm not used to it.'

'We're here for seven days,' Mum told him. 'It's a lovely place, Vlad, an island with palm trees and beaches and lots of corals and beautiful fishes to look at. It's idyllic, it's what everyone dreams of.'

'It's not what vampires dream of, I can tell you. We dream of high mountains with ice-capped peaks and remote castles full of bats and spiders' webs, and people all ready to be vampirised. I don't feel comfortable here, not a bit like myself.'

'There's nothing I can do about it, Vlad. We've booked for a week and a week we will stay and you'll have to put up with it.'

Vlad brightened up. 'I know, I'll look after the Snoglet. I'd enjoy that. It would give me something to do. I'll be the vampire nanny.'

'That would be lovely for me,' said Mum dubiously, 'but are you sure you can manage?'

'Manage? Manage? Of course I can manage – I'm the father of five, remember. Manage indeed! Now, off you go and do funny peoply things like swimming in the ocean and looking at fishes and frying yourself in the sun. Go on, don't hang about.'

'Thanks, Vlad,' Mum called over her shoulder as she ran off to join the others snorkelling in the water.

At the end of the day the Stones ran along the beach towards Vlad, dripping wet and glowing with health and excitement.

'It was fantastic, Vlad,' Paul told him. 'Thousands of fishes with amazing patterns on them.'

'Really,' commented Vlad sourly.

'You'd love it, Vlad,' enthused Judy. 'I wish you'd come into the water. You're missing out, you really are.'

'Someone has to be responsible and look after the Snoglet, someone has to be restrained and not go potty about a few silly fish.'

'Zoe looks very happy,' commented Mum. 'You've done a good job, Vlad. Now I'd better feed her.'

'She's been fed.'

'Then I'd better change her.'

'She's been changed.'

'Then I'll bath her.'

'She's been bathed.'

The Stones all stared at Vlad.

'I don't know what you four are gawping at. You're even beginning to look like fish. Why shouldn't I be able to look after one baby? I've got five of my own, remember. Now, off you go and get changed. You can't go in to supper dripping wet like that. Go on, Zoe is asleep and I am trying hard to do a bit of studying.'

'What do you mean "studying", Vlad? I thought we were supposed to be on holiday.'

'You may well be on holiday, but I am busy doing my homework on endangered species and I am not happy with what I am discovering. People, honestly, they're hopeless. I think you should look at ways of not turning into a person, Judy.'

'Why, Vlad, what have people done now?'

'Oh, nothing much, just messed up the whole planet,

that's all. Honestly, Judy, it's very upsetting; the seas are polluted, and so is the air and the rivers, and the forests are being cut down, and affected by chemical diseases, and who's doing all this? Not vampires but people, of course. However, inevitably, vampires and animals are suffering the consequences as well.'

'I know there's lots of pollution,' said Judy, 'but it can't be as bad as all that.'

'Jolly well is,' replied Vlad indignantly, 'and all these endangered species I'm supposed to be helping – they're only endangered because of people. Just look at this list I've made: it's a disgrace. The eagle dying out due to destruction of forests. Leopards hunted for their skins. Tigers' habitat destroyed and skins valued as trophies. Crocodiles sought after because their skins are fashionable for handbags.'

'But, Vlad, crocodiles are on the increase again, remember?'

'Oh yes, so they are. Oh well, isn't that just like people? Rescue a really horrible creature like those unfriendly crocodiles but continue to hunt the poor old whale who sings so nicely. And do you know why people are hunting whales? For cosmetics. I mean, I ask you.'

'Lots of people are worried about whales,' interrupted Judy indignantly. Vlad ignored her and carried on with his tirade.

'Then there's a large number of Australian species threatened. Right here, on this very continent: the pelican and parrots and the hairy nosed wombat. It's enough to make you weep.'

'I see what you mean, Vlad. When you realise the scale of the problem it really is depressing.'

'It most certainly is, and that list is just a few of the animals which are threatened and that's before you

even begin to think about vampires. You know, Great Uncle Ghitza probably had the right attitude to people: vampirise 'em and have done. No messing about, no half measures. I'm very upset, Judy, very upset indeed.'

'Poor Vlad,' said Judy sympathetically. 'It is very worrying, but what are you going to do about it?'

'I don't know yet, Judy, but I'm thinking. As the only representative of an endangered species who can talk to people, I have a special responsibility. I'll come up with something, don't you worry. I'll think of a way of making a bit of a splash. And that's a promise!'

Judy felt decidedly uneasy and made a mental note to discuss the matter with her parents and Paul. As a temporary measure she decided to divert Vlad.

'Come and have some supper, Vlad. Everyone on the island is asking about you and wants to meet you. They're all waiting for you in the dining room.'

'Oh really?' said Vlad brightening up. 'I can't disappoint my public, even if they are people. Go on, you get changed and then we'll make a grand entrance.'

When the Stones went into the dining room, everyone greeted Vlad and wanted their photograph taken with him.

'It's very boring,' Vlad whispered to Paul, 'having my picture taken all the time, but it wouldn't do to disappoint them – so I'll smile and pretend I enjoy it.'

After supper it was announced that there would be a sing-song. One of the diving instructors came up to Vlad.

'G'day, Vlad, I'm Clint. I hear you're a bonzer piano player.'

'A what?' demanded Vlad.

'A bonzer piano player.'

'If you think you can insult me and get away with it, young man, you're very much mistaken. I've a good mind to vampirise you. A bonzer piano player indeed.'

'Eh, bonzer means very good.'

'Oh,' said Vlad. 'I see, more strine.'

'Too right, mate.'

'Yes, you have been correctly informed, I am a bonzer piano player.'

'Well, would you like to give us a bit of a show tonight?'

'Why not?' agreed Vlad. 'I need to get some practice for my two big concerts. You're on, Clint.'

So later that evening Vlad raced up and down the piano, leaping and diving and jumping up and down. The audience enjoyed it enormously.

'I shall be playing like that in two special concerts,' Vlad told them, 'to raise money for endangered species and people will pay a lot of money to get in. So you lot have done well to hear me for free. Would you like to hear some of my special vampire songs?'

'Yes!' yelled the audience. So with Dad at the piano Vlad sang *The Lament for Great Uncle Ghitza* and then wanted everyone to join in the chorus of his next song.

'It's my vampire version of that popular old Irish tune *Sweet Molly Malone*. Now, as lots of you Aussies are of Irish stock, I'm sure you'll join in and make a lot of noise.' And he sang

> *In Sydney's fair city,*
> *Where vampires are witty,*
> *There once lived a vampire.*
> *His name Vlad the Drac.*
> *He goes with his van,*
> *Wherever he can,*
> *Crying humans and people,*
> *Alive, alive-oh.*

And everyone joined in the chorus:

> *Alive, alive-oh,*
> *Alive, alive-oh.*
> *Crying humans and people,*
> *Alive, alive-oh.*

When it was over Vlad decided he was exhausted.

'You sing me an Australian song now,' he said. 'Fair's fair.'

'Right,' said Clint. 'I'll just tune my guitar and we'll sing *Waltzing Matilda* for Vlad.'

Vlad sat on the edge of Zoe's cot and got ready to listen. Clint began to strum his guitar and sang:

Once a jolly swagman camped by a billabong,
Under the shade of a coolabah tree,
And he sang as he watched and waited till his billy boiled,
'Who'll come a-waltzing Matilda with me?'

and everyone joined in the chorus:

'Waltzing Matilda, Waltzing Matilda,
Who'll come a-waltzing Matilda with me,'
And he sang as he watched and waited till his billy boiled,
'Who'll come a-waltzing Matilda with me.'

As the song went on Vlad looked more and more miserable and finally climbed under a sheet and buried his head in a blanket. When the song was over everyone clapped and cheered. Clint looked over towards the cot.

'Did you like that, Vlad?' he began and then tailed off. 'Where's he gone? He was there a minute ago.'

Mum pulled back the sheet and there was Vlad cowering, shaking with fright.

'What's up, Vlad?' asked Mum. 'Stop being silly and come on out.'

'Too scared,' whispered Vlad.

'But why?' asked Mum puzzled.

'I don't want to come out 'cos Australians are cannibals.'

'Cannibals?! Don't be silly, Vlad, what a crazy idea.'

'Jolly well are,' mumbled Vlad.

'Do you know what cannibal means?'

'It means people who eat other people.'

'But whatever gives you the idea that Australians are into that?'

'It's all in that song they sing, *Waltzing Matilda*.'

'I honestly don't know what you're on about, Vlad. It's a song about a sheep thief not a cannibal.'

'That's what you think,' answered Vlad. 'But you tell me this – is William a boy's name or is it not?'

'Well, yes, it is.'

'And is Billy short for William or is it not?'

'Yes, it is.'

'So in the song when the sheep thief is waiting till his Billy boiled, is he or is he not smacking his lips until he can eat poor Billy for his tea?'

Judy burst out laughing.

'Oh, Vlad, you are funny! No, he was waiting till the kettle boiled. A camping kettle is called a billy.'

Vlad looked unconvinced.

'That's what you say but I think you've been conned. And I must say, while all people are pretty odd, Australian women take the biscuit. I mean, how any Australian woman can be persuaded to call her son William, I shall never be able to comprehend, not even if I live to be a thousand years old.'

The next morning Vlad sat under a tree next to Zoe, wearing his shorts and hat with corks bobbing around. The Stones came out dressed in flippers and masks for snorkelling. Vlad sniffed disapprovingly.

'You all look ridiculous, going to all that trouble just to look at a few silly fishes.'

Clint came up to join them.

'Hi, Vlado! Can't I persuade you to come into the

104

water and have at least a little look at all the fishes and the coral? Seems a shame to come all this way and not see the reef.'

'Apart from anything else,' Vlad informed him, 'you wouldn't catch me dressing up in all that silly gear and anyway you don't have anything small enough for me.'

'That's true. Just leave it with me, Vlado.'

'What's all this Vlado stuff?' demanded the vampire.

'Oh, it's something Australians do to their friends, call them Johnno, or Stevo or Jacko – just friendly.'

'Ah,' said Vlad smiling. 'All right, Clinto, you'd better take Mumo and Dado and Judo and Paulo into the water and leave me to take care of Snogleto and write cards to my children in Romanio – I mean Romania.'

Vlad was busy writing a card to his son Ghitza, when Clint ran up to him.

'I solved the problem of you looking at the fish, Vlad. Look!'

In his hand Clint had a see-through plastic bottle with a cork in the neck and a straw going through the cork. On it was written *Vlad's submarine*. Clint was glowing with pride.

'Well, Vlad, what do you say to that?'

'No, thank you,' said Vlad politely, 'I prefer dry land.'

'Nothing to be scared of,' Clint assured him. 'It'll be as safe as houses. The bottle will bob around on the top of the water and you can lie down and look out of it and breathe through the straw. You'll be quite safe.'

'I'm not scared,' Vlad told him. 'Oh dear me, no. We vampires are a fearless lot. Sharks, crocodiles, poisonous snakes, none of them worry me. I just can't

105

be bothered, that's all.'

'I think you're scared,' taunted Clint.

'Great Uncle Ghitza would disown you if he were here,' pressed Judy.

'Vampires aren't used to the sea,' said Mum. 'It's natural that Vlad is nervous.'

'I'm not nervous,' insisted Vlad. 'It's just that I've got better things to do.'

'Come off it,' said Paul. 'There's nothing better to do on the Barrier Reef – you're a scaredy cat.'

'Why not just admit it?' sneered Dad.

'Bring on the submarine,' commanded Vlad, standing up to his full height. 'I'll show you silly people what vampires are made of.'

'You'll love it,' Dad assured him.

'It's magic,' agreed Judy.

'Best thing ever,' added Paul.

'If you get scared,' said Mum, 'just raise your right hand and we'll pull the submarine out of the water at once.'

'Vampires never get scared,' Vlad informed her. 'We don't know the meaning of the word. Now, if I don't return, here is my will leaving everything to Mrs Vlad and the children and please see to it that my earthly remains are returned to Romania to rest beside those of Great Uncle Ghitza and please explain to Magda that I died to redeem the honour of the vampires.'

Then he solemnly shook hands with each of the Stones and climbed reluctantly into the bottle and put the straw into his mouth.

'I'll just lower you into the water for one minute at first, while you get used to it,' said Clint, 'then two minutes. All right?'

'All right, skipper,' said Vlad. Slowly the bottle was

lowered. A minute later Clint lifted it up and opened the cork.

'All right, Vlad?'

'All right! It's fantastic. All these little fish, hundreds of them all darting around between the coral. They're wonderful colours, yellow and black stripes and bright pink ones, all shapes and colours. Quick, I want to go down again. It's like fairy land. Come on,' he called to the Stones. 'It's great, nothing to be afraid of.'

Back on the beach a couple of hours later, Vlad sat telling Zoe all about it.

'You know, Snogleto, it's a real shame that you're too little to go in,' he told her. 'It's a whole new world under there. My children would love it. I'll have to think about a family holiday here in Australia, I definitely will.'

'Sounds like you're getting to like Australia after all, Vlad,' said Judy smiling.

'To be perfectly honest with you, Judy, I am. It's not at all as I expected and they certainly appreciate vampires here. No, I must admit Australia has been a very pleasant surprise.'

'Dad'll be relieved when I tell him – he's been worried about your not liking it and being miserable.'

'Don't you dare tell him, Judy. Don't you dare. I've got my reputation as a champion Rommie Whinger to protect. I've got to have something to carry on and whinge about. Promise you won't tell.'

'All right,' sighed Judy, 'but I think you're being silly.'

After that Clint took Vlad out in the submarine every day and they became firm friends. One evening Clint took Vlad for a walk round the island and Vlad told him all about the work he'd been doing on endangered species.

'It's a good job you're doing there, Vlado,' Clint told him. 'I mean, lots of us are worried about the environment. I'm a greenie myself.'

'No, you're not,' said Vlad indignantly. '*I'm* green but you're a sort of sludgy, peoply shade of light brown.'

'No, you drongo, not green in colour, green in my sympathies.'

'I don't follow,' frowned Vlad.

'There are lots of people all over the world who are concerned about the sorts of things we've been talking about – particularly the destruction of the rainforests in Australia. We call ourselves green because we're on the side of green things like trees and grass.'

'And vampires?'

'Yes, I suppose so.'

'Good,' said Vlad, 'because vampires may have vampirised a few people here and there, but we never, ever, did as much damage as people.'

'You'd better join the Greens then, Vlad.'

'I most certainly will. You know, it seems to me that the time has come for green vampires and green people to join forces.'

'Great idea, Vlad, and as you're quite a celebrity maybe you could do something to draw people's attention to the problem.'

'Humm,' agreed Vlad, 'I'm very good at getting attention – and I've got a few ideas brewing, so you just be prepared for Vlad the Drac, the greatest, greenest vampire in the world to act.'

8

BEYOND THE BLACK STUMP

'Where are we going now?' demanded Vlad. 'It's very hot and I don't feel like sitting in a stuffy old car day after day yet again.'

'Vlad, please don't start whinging,' said Mum. 'It's very hot for all of us.'

'Why do we have to go in this rotten old car anyway? Why can't we just fly everywhere?'

'Because we can't afford it,' Mum told him firmly.

'Anyway,' Judy chipped in, 'we see more of Australia this way. It's fun.'

'Speak for yourself,' sniffed Vlad. 'It's all the same, just lots of gum trees and when you've seen one, you've seen them all.'

'I like it,' declared Paul. 'It's fun travelling around and I'm fed up listening to you being a Rommie Whinger.'

'Poor old Vlad, poor little Drac,' complained the vampire. 'I want to be in the mountains surrounded by snow and forests. I can't stand the heat and the flies and I'm thirsty.'

'We're all hot and thirsty, Vlad,' Judy pointed out, 'but there's no point in carrying on about it.'

'I'm thirsty and I want a drink now,' insisted Vlad sulkily.

'You can't have one till we stop,' Dad told him firmly. 'And if you're going to go on like this all day I shall put a gag on you.'

'I think you are all horrible,' sniffed Vlad. 'And I want to go and sit in the boot: it might be cooler and it will certainly be more peaceful. Would you stop and let me get into the back, please.'

'With pleasure!' said Dad and he drew up at the side of the road and opened the back for Vlad to get in. The Stones enjoyed the rest of the day. They played games in the car and sang and listened to tapes and munched fruit and enjoyed the beautiful scenery. Towards evening there was a magnificent sunset.

'Better start looking for somewhere to stay,' said Mum. 'A caravan park or a camping site, if we can't find a motel.'

'We're a long way from anywhere, aren't we?' commented Judy. 'We've hardly seen a farm or another car for a couple of hours.'

'We are out in the outback,' Dad informed her. ' "Beyond the Black Stump." It's vast and it's very thinly populated, far more sheep and cows than people.'

'You're very low on petrol, Nick,' Mum reminded him.

'No worries,' he told her smiling. 'I put two large cans in the boot. It's not a good idea to travel in the outback without spare petrol. I'd better stop and put some in the tank while it's still light.'

So Dad stopped the car and they all got out to stretch their legs and admire the scenery and the sunset. Dad opened the back of the car and there lay Vlad fast asleep. Dad quietly picked up one of the petrol cans.

'It's empty,' he cried in horror, 'and so's the other one! Oh no! Vlad, wake up.'

Vlad stetched and yawned. 'What's all the fuss about?'

'What have you done with all the petrol?' yelled Dad.

'Drunk it, of course,' said Vlad. 'Isn't that what it's for?'

'Of all the damn fool things to do,' shouted Dad. 'Vlad's drunk all our spare petrol. Now we're stuck on this road a million miles from anywhere and it's about to get dark. Honestly, Vlad, haven't you any sense?'

'Quieten down, Nick,' said Mum, 'and let's think of the best thing to do. Maybe we should spend the night here. We've got the tents in the car.'

'It's too dark to put the tents up now,' Dad told her,. 'and we haven't got any water. We'll just have to sit here and wait and hope that someone drives past in the next two days. If not, we're in serious trouble.'

'Sorry,' sniffed Vlad miserably, 'I didn't realise.'

'I wish I'd told Sir Tibor to keep you and keep his job,' fumed Dad. 'We could be here for days. We could all die of thirst and hunger.'

'Didn't mean to cause all this trouble,' whispered Vlad.

They huddled miserably together at the side of the road and tried to ignore the mosquitos that buzzed around.

'How long do you think we'll have to wait here?' asked Judy.

'We may have to spend the night here,' said Dad grimly, 'and when it gets light I'll start walking and try to find a farm or a telephone box or something.'

'I'm not sure that would be a good idea,' interrupted Mum, in a worried voice. 'They tell you to stay by your car if it breaks down.'

'I can't just sit here and let you all starve,' insisted Dad.

Just then they heard the sound of an engine in the

distance. Mum rushed and turned on the car lights. Dad, Vlad and the children jumped up and down and yelled. A truck drew up and a weatherbeaten man jumped out. In the trailer behind his truck a dog barked vigorously.

'G'day,' he said. 'You broken down or something?'

'No,' said Dad, 'we're out of petrol.'

'Don't you know better than to go driving round the bush without a spare can, mate? You Pommies, no damn sense.'

'We had two spare cans,' Paul told him indignantly.

'Yes, but I drank them,' Vlad told him proudly, climbing on to Paul's shoulder.

'Well,' said the man, 'my oath, it's Vlad the Drac. Well now, what do you know! I never met anyone I saw on telly before.'

Vlad beamed with pride but as the dog's barking got louder, he climbed into Judy's pocket and peeped out.

'I see you've got a baby, too,' said the man. 'Gawd, it was a bit of luck for you my coming along this way. You'd better come and spend the night at my place. Can't leave you out here. Come on, Mrs, you and the baby get up in the front with me and the rest of you into the trailer. Don't worry about Laddie. He just makes a lot of noise.'

'Can I come in the front with you?' Vlad asked nervously. 'I'm sure that horrible dog wants to eat me.'

'This is all your fault, so be quiet,' said Judy.

'The name's Harry Wilks,' the man told them. 'I live about half an hour down the track. I'll drive you back here tomorrow morning with a couple of cans of petrol and you can be off on your way.'

'We're very grateful,' Mum told him.

'No worries,' said Harry cheerfully. 'I couldn't leave yous by the roadside, now could I? This is quite an event for me. We lead a quiet life round here and I've never met a vampire before.'

'You should try to keep it that way,' Dad told him.

When they arrived at the sheep station Harry introduced them to his wife.

'I'm June,' she said, 'and it's a real pleasure to have you here. I'm from England myself, from Yorkshire. Came out just after the war with my family, when I was only fourteen. So it's nice for me to meet someone from the old country. You all go and have a nice shower and then come down and have a drink on the verandah.'

So a while later they were all sitting round sipping cold drinks. Vlad was given a glass of sheep dip and was sipping away when he suddenly let out a shriek.

'Something bit me,' he squeaked.

'Yeah, the mozzies are bad at this time of year,' said June. 'Don't worry, Vlad, they only take a bit of blood.'

'Like vampires?' asked Vlad.

'Yes, I suppose so,' agreed June.

Vlad scratched away. 'At least vampires have the good manners not to leave a nasty itch.'

'Don't worry, Vlad,' said Harry. 'I'm just going to make a barbie, that will drive the mozzies away.'

'What's a barbie?' enquired Vlad.

'A barbecue. Don't you have them in Romania? You make a fire outdoors and cook meat and things over the flame or in the coals. Tastes really good.'

'I got out some steaks and some hamburgers and some sausages,' said June. 'That suit everyone?'

'Yes,' chorused the Stones.

'No,' said Vlad sourly.

114

'No worries. I've got you a nice bar of soap,' she told Vlad.

'Thanks,' said Vlad, and flew over to watch Harry getting the barbecue going. The Stones sat on the balcony and sipped their drinks and chatted to June Wilks, who was delighted to have company and enjoyed playing with Zoe. Suddenly they all began to sniff.

'What's that funny smell?' said Paul.

They all sniffed hard.

'It is odd, isn't it?' said June. 'Harry, what's that smell?'

'It's the bar of soap,' called Harry. 'Vlad must have put it on the grill when I wasn't looking.'

'Oh no! Just look at it,' moaned Judy. 'Soap everywhere and I was so looking forward to that steak. Now all our steaks will taste of soap.'

'You'll just have to be generous with the fried onions and the ketchup,' laughed Harry. 'He's a character, that Vlad.'

'I want onions and ketchup on my bar of soap too,' insisted Vlad. So Harry put the bar of soap in a bun and smothered it with onions and ketchup and gave it to Vlad, who munched away contentedly. Soon they were all sitting round and eating big steaks and baked potatoes and trying to ignore the soapy tinge to everything.

'It is a bit much for me,' Vlad informed them, 'would anyone like to finish mine?' Everyone politely declined. 'Funny,' said Vlad, 'I thought people liked barbecues.'

The next morning Harry drove them back to their car and filled up the tank for them.

'It's about an hour to the next petrol station,' he told them. 'You'll have no more problems.'

'Vlad,' Dad said sternly, 'you are going to sit in the

116

car with us and you are not going to eat or drink one thing without asking permission, is that clear?'

'All right,' groaned Vlad. 'Poor old Vlad, poor little Drac.'

'Thanks so much for everything,' said Mum. 'I don't know what would have happened to us if you hadn't come along. It was lovely to meet you. We've all really enjoyed it.'

'Yes indeed,' said Dad shaking Harry's hand. 'It's been most interesting to see a real Australian sheep station. If you ever come to England, look us up.'

'And if you ever come to Romania, look me up,' Vlad told him. 'I'll make sure that my son Dad doesn't vampirise you.'

'Well, thanks,' said Harry. 'I've been promising June a trip overseas, back to Yorkshire and that, so I might just take you all up on the offer.'

They all waved enthusiastically to Harry as they drove away.

'You see,' Vlad told them, 'I did you a favour. Instead of staying in some boring motel we stayed on a real outback farm and met nice people and had a new experience and all for free. Yes, you should definitely be grateful to me for drinking the petrol.'

The next night they stopped at the camping site in Warrumbungle National Park.

'What is a national park anyway?' asked Vlad.

'It's an area of outstanding natural beauty that is preserved for people to enjoy. You can't have industry or mining or lots of buildings in a national park,' Paul told him.

'This one's a nature reserve too,' added Judy, 'so

there are lots of animals around and no one is allowed to kill them.'

'Wild animals!' cried Vlad in alarm. 'We might be eaten in our beds while we sleep.'

'Come on, Vlad,' Paul told him. 'You should know better than that with all the reading you've been doing. Australian animals don't eat people.'

'Crocodiles do,' sniffed Vlad.

'They're not around here, they're much further north, so don't worry about it.'

'In that case these national parks sound like a good idea,' commented Vlad. 'I'm surprised people thought of it.'

The Stones breathed in the fresh air and looked round at the volcanic mountains and the thick forests.

'Isn't it wonderful?' said Judy. 'Not like anything I expected.'

'Come on,' said Dad. 'Stop looking around and help me get the tents up before it gets dark.'

So while Mum looked after Zoe, Dad and Judy put the tents up and Paul began to stoke the barbecue fire on the site. Vlad surveyed the busy scene sourly.

'I hope you don't expect me to sleep in one of those things,' he announced, looking at the tents.

'You may sleep wherever you like,' Dad told him, 'but we're tired and we're going to bed.'

That night they all slept soundly in the tents. As soon as it got light Vlad woke up.

'Wakey, wakey!' he shouted at Judy and Paul. 'Come on, rise and shine. Up you get, can't loaf around in the sleeping bag all day.'

'Get lost!' snapped Paul.

'Go 'way,' yawned Judy.

'Quiet, you'll wake the baby up,' whispered Mum.

Dad just snored.

Vlad sighed and went and sat outside and complained to himself.

'Poor old Vlad, poor little Drac. Nothing to do, people are boring,' and he began to play with the tent pegs. Suddenly Judy and Paul's tent collapsed.

'Help!' Vlad yelled from under the canvas.

Dad staggered sleepily out of his tent to see what was going on. Just as he put his hand to his head in horror at the sight of the fallen tent, his own tent caved in.

'What happened?' gasped Judy.

'Some idiot pulled the tent pegs out,' growled Paul.

'Vlad,' shouted Dad, 'come here.'

'I told you tents weren't a sensible place to sleep,' Vlad told them smugly. 'A whiff of a breeze and they're down like a pack of cards.'

'Wind had nothing to do with it. You pulled up the tent pegs.'

'I was bored with everyone asleep but I didn't pull the tents down.'

'It's the pegs that keep the tents up,' yelled Dad.

'How was I to know that it was only those silly old pegs that kept your rotten tents up?'

'I can't stand it,' fumed Dad. 'Now, Vlad, will you just go away somewhere, far from the tents so that we can clear up the mess without further mishap. Just go away. Don't bother anyone or do anything.'

'Poor old Vlad,' muttered the vampire. 'How was I to know 'bout the silly tents? Poor little Drac.' And he walked away sulkily into a clump of trees.

When the tents were finally unravelled and packed away in the car and the Stones had eaten breakfast, Judy looked round for Vlad.

'Vlad,' she called, 'we're going. Come on out.'

'He's sulking,' said Dad. 'Vlad, come here right

119

now or we'll go without you.'

There was no reply, so they all went and searched the clearing. They saw several kangaroos leaping around but no Vlad.

'Dad,' said Paul, 'I think Vlad may have gone off in a kangaroo pouch. He did that in London Zoo and enjoyed it.'

'We'll never find him if he's done that,' cried Judy. 'He could be anywhere in the bush. Poor Vlad, he'll be so scared.'

'We'd better go and tell the ranger who runs this national park,' sighed Mum. 'He may tell us what to do.'

So they drove to the ranger's hut and told him what had happened. The ranger rubbed his head.

'You're going to have one hell of a problem finding him, a little chap like that. I don't even know where to suggest that you begin.'

'Supposing some Aborigines found him,' burst out Judy, 'and they didn't have a television and didn't know who he was. They might hurt him.'

'Now that's one thing you don't have to worry about,' the ranger assured her. 'Mostly they have TV for one thing, but for another they have a different set of attitudes to the earth and life. They would just accept him as another creature with a right to be here. They won't harm him.'

'What do you think we should do?' asked Mum.

'Not much you can do. I'll phone round all the local police stations and the other rangers. Then if he does turn up somewhere they'll know where you are. Make yourself some coffee while I make the calls.'

After about ten calls the ranger turned to them.

'One of the other rangers noticed another camper. He's gone over to ask him if he's seen your vampire and then he'll call back.'

About twenty minutes later the phone rang and the ranger answered.

'Thank goodness for that. He's having breakfast with the camper. Travelled by kangaroo, did he? Yeah? We guessed as much. That is a relief. Thanks for your trouble, mate. We'll get over there right away.'

'We've found him,' the ranger told them. 'Come on. I'll lead the way and you follow in your car.'

Half an hour later they reached a remote part of the national park. Sitting by a stream were a young black man and Vlad, deeply engrossed in conversation.

'Oh hello,' said Vlad casually, as the Stones rushed up.

'We've been so worried about you,' burst out Judy.

'That was unnecessary,' said Vlad. 'Now please sit down and be quiet. This is my friend Charlie Moreton and we're having a very interesting conversation.'

'Vlad, how dare you just wander off like that?' began Dad.

'Be quiet!' Vlad told him. 'And sit down and listen. Charlie's been telling me such fascinating things about the aboriginal people. All about how they came out of the Dream Time, and I've been telling him all about vampires and Great Uncle Ghitza and things.'

'Nightmare time,' muttered Dad.

'Trust you to trivialise things,' snapped Vlad. 'This is a serious matter. And he's been telling me how his people nearly became extinct but they saved themselves and there are more of them now. So that's very encouraging.'

'Yeah, the little green fella and I found plenty to talk about, isn't that right, Vlad?'

'Certainly is, black fella.'

'Vlad,' said Mum, 'you shouldn't call him that.'

'Why not, Mrs? That's what I am and proud of it,' said Charlie.

'We really understand each other,' chipped in Vlad, 'because they believe people should respect the land and the water and the air and *all* the creatures that live in the world.'

'That's right,' said Charlie Moreton. 'They've got as much right to be here as we have.'

'I'm very impressed,' said Vlad. 'It's been a most informative morning. I'm beginning to discover that some people have the right ideas. I feel much more hopeful about the endangered species because so many people do seem to be worried about it.'

'Keep up the good fight, Vlad,' Charlie Moreton told him.

'I will, mate, don't worry.'

'Vlad, we're going to have to go. It's a very late start as it is,' Dad told him. 'Charlie, can we give you a lift somewhere?'

'Thanks, but no. I'm on foot, walking round here. These used to be my tribal lands, where my mob used to hang out. I'm at uni in Sydney but I like to come back and get the feel of the place.'

'Charlie feels about this place like I do about Transylvania,' commented Vlad. 'It's where vampires feel they belong, so however lovely some other place is, it will never feel quite the same as the Carpathian mountains.'

'You're not wrong,' said Charlie. 'And I'd like to give you a memento of our meeting. I carve boomerangs for a hobby. Would you like one?'

'It's very pretty,' said Vlad, looking at the carved and painted wood. 'What is it for?'

'It's a weapon. You throw it at an animal and if it doesn't hit the animal it comes back to you.'

'That's silly,' sniffed Vlad. 'If you throw a stick away it stays away unless some silly dog brings it back. Look, I'll show you.'

He flung the boomerang across the grass as far as he could.

'You see,' he said turning triumphantly towards the cluster of people watching. 'It doesn't come back.'

'Look out!' yelled Charlie Moreton.

They all threw themselves flat on the ground except Vlad. The boomerang sailed through the air and hit Vlad on the head. He lay there motionless.

'He's not bleeding,' said Charlie Moreton bending over Vlad with a worried look on his face. 'He's just out for the count.'

'Just the way I like him,' grinned Dad.

'Let me take a look,' said Mum. 'I'm a doctor,' she told Charlie, as she bent down and prodded Vlad a bit.

'You're right,' she told Charlie Moreton. 'It's not serious, he'll come round in a while but he'll have a sore head.'

'Take good care of him,' said Charlie.

'We will,' Judy assured him. 'Goodbye. It's been super meeting you. Enjoy the rest of the holiday.'

'I will, and say goodbye to the little green fella for me.'

'We will,' called the Stones, and they drove away waving to Charlie, until he was just a speck on the horizon.

9

UP THE CREEK

They drove fast down the straight highway until they came to a small town.

'Let's stop here and have a drink,' suggested Mum, 'and buy some fruit and things for the trip,'

'Fine,' agreed Dad. 'I've got something special to buy. I'll join you in the café over there.'

'Don't you think we ought to take Vlad to the hospital?' Judy asked her mother. 'Just in case he's broken something.'

'He's all right,' Mum assured her. 'I checked. He'll just be unconscious for a while and then have a sore head when he wakes up. There's really nothing to worry about and, as you may remember, Vlad isn't too keen on hospitals.'

'I hope you're right,' muttered Judy, sipping her Coke. Just then Dad returned carrying a big parcel and humming cheerfully to himself.

'Whatever is it?' asked Paul.

Dad ripped off the paper and with a flourish displayed a large bird cage.

'Vlad's new home,' he declared.

'You can't do that to Vlad!' said Judy. 'It would be like putting him in prison and it would be humiliating.'

'Judy,' said Dad severely, 'over the last twenty-four hours, Vlad has risked our lives by drinking all the petrol and leaving us stranded in the middle of nowhere. He got us all in an anxiety state by getting lost and then nearly gets himself killed with a boomerang. He won't listen to what anyone tells him. For his own sake he needs to be protected, and I want to enjoy what is left of this holiday.'

'I agree with Dad,' said Paul.

'Me too,' said Mum reluctantly, 'but it's a very big cage. Where will we put it?'

'I thought Judy could have it on her knee since she's so fond of Vlad.'

'All right,' said Judy.

So still unconscious, Vlad was put in the cage and Judy sat with him on her knee in the back of the car.

'Where is our next stop?' asked Paul as they cruised along.

'We're making for Canberra,' Mum told him. 'You remember Aunt Louise? She lives there and we're all invited.'

'Great Aunt Louise, Gran's sister?' asked Paul.

'Umm,' said Dad. 'She emigrated to Australia thirty years ago. It'll be nice to live in a house again and not in a tent or a motel.'

'Have you warned her about Vlad?' asked Judy.

'Of course,' said Mum. 'We wouldn't just turn up with him. But Gran had written to her telling her all about Vlad and the TV broadcast and Aunt Louise is really keen to meet him.'

'Hmmm,' commented Dad. 'How long do you give her before she begs us to take him away?'

'She may like him,' Judy pointed out. 'Gran did.'

'I know,' sighed Dad. 'And I always thought my mother was such a sensible woman.'

In the middle of the next day Vlad began to stir and moan on his stretcher. After a while he sat up and looked around.

'Where am I?' he asked.

'You're in a cage,' Judy told him. 'You got knocked

out by a boomerang and you've been unconscious for a couple of days.'

'Why am I in a cage?' demanded Vlad. 'Let me out this instant.'

'No way,' Dad told him. 'You're a danger and a menace, Vlad, to yourself and to us and for the rest of this trip you stay in that cage.'

'Poor old Vlad, poor little Drac,' muttered the vampire fiercely.

'What a relief,' said Mum. 'If he's saying that he can't be too badly injured. Do you want something to eat, Vlad?'

'Pretty Polly,' replied Vlad. 'How's your father? Yo, heave ho and a bottle of rum, fifteen men on a dead man's chest.'

'His mind's been affected by the blow,' sighed Dad.

'Not at all,' snapped Vlad badtemperedly. 'I am merely talking like a parrot because I'm being treated like one. Still, parrots are an endangered species too, so maybe it's a good idea for me to have this experience. Poor old Polly, poor little parrot.'

As they approached Canberra Vlad asked, 'Exactly where are we going now?'

'We are going to stay with Aunt Louise,' Mum explained. 'She lives in Canberra, which is the capital of Australia, and she's invited us to stay for a week or so.'

'And who is Aunt Louise when she's at home?' demanded Vlad.

'She's Gran's sister,' Judy told him. 'You remember Gran?'

'I most certainly do,' said Vlad. 'She was a nice lady, even if she did have the misfortune to be the Lord High's mater. So this lady is the Lord High's mater's sister?'

'That's right,' said Dad grimly, 'and you jolly well behave while we're there or you can spend the whole week in the cage.'

In fact Aunt Louise was delighted to see Vlad.

'I saw you on television,' she told him, 'and I've been so looking forward to your visit. But I didn't realise you lived in a cage.'

'I don't,' Vlad assured her. 'It's just that the Lord High, eh, I mean Dad, insisted that I go in one. A quite unnecessary precaution and I'm very fed up with it.'

'I'm not surprised,' said Aunt Louise. 'I'm shocked to find you behaving like this, Nick. Let Vlad out at once.'

So Vlad was released and began to fly around cheerfully.'

'I never realised how important being free was,' he cried as he flew round the house five times. 'Let's go out and do something. We've all been stuck in that car for days.'

'Where would you like to go?' asked Aunt Louise. 'How about going down to the river for a swim? You can hire canoes and things down there as well.'

'Sounds great!' said the children.

'I'll stay at home with Zoe,' said Mum. 'It's a bit hot for the baby and I'd like a rest. You'll go, won't you, Nick?'

'Sure,' said Dad, 'but I'd be much happier if Vlad went back in his cage.'

'Don't be silly, Nick,' said Aunt Louise sharply. 'Of course Vlad won't go back in his cage. I just don't understand this bee you've got in your bonnet about Vlad.'

'You will, Aunt Louise. By tonight, you will understand me very well.'

When they got to the river the children and Dad rushed into the water and swam around, splashing each other and shrieking with delight.

'Aren't you going in too?' Aunt Louise asked Vlad.

'It looks a bit rough and cold,' Vlad told her.

'Yes, it's quite a dangerous river,' she told him. 'It's got waterfalls and rapids. Once you get into the wrong current you just get carried along.'

'Shouldn't we warn Judy and Paul?' asked Vlad anxiously. 'Leave that horrible Dad to his fate, but we must warn the children.'

'Oh, don't worry about it, Vlad. It's quite safe at this point. It's further downstream where the canoeing goes on that the current is dangerous.'

'What's canoeing?' asked Vlad.

'I'll show you,' said Aunt Louise. 'Come on.'

So sitting on her shoulder Vlad walked up to the top of a cliff. There, down below, were people in canoes with paddles sailing merrily down the river.

'Umm, that looks like fun,' said the vampire. 'When Judy comes out of the water I'll ask her to go canoeing with me.'

They went back to the spot where they had left their things and arrived just as the Stones were coming out of the water.

'It's lovely in there,' said Dad. 'Very warm, perfect for swimming.'

'They're canoeing further down,' said Vlad. 'I want to go in a canoe. Will you come with me, Judy?'

'No!' said Dad quickly. 'There'll be a disaster.'

'Nonsense, Nick,' said Aunt Louise. 'It's not dangerous if people are sensible and wear life jackets. Let the children have a go. They seem sensible enough and they aren't babies any more.'

So, with misgiving, Dad gave his permission. Vlad

MINI HAHA ★

went in the canoe with Judy.

'Be careful!' yelled Dad from the bank.

'This is fun, isn't it?' Vlad said to Judy. 'Can I paddle for a bit?'

'I think you should leave it to me,' Judy told him. 'The paddle is too big for you to cope with.'

'Nonsense,' said Vlad. 'Give it to me this minute. Come on, Judy, I want to paddle my own canoe.'

Reluctantly, Judy handed it to him. 'It's only for a minute,' she told him.

Vlad began to paddle furiously but the paddle was so much bigger than him that the canoe stayed still for a moment, then began to turn round in circles and finally turned over. Judy quickly surfaced in her life jacket and swam for the shore. As she climbed out of the water she saw a speck of green disappear over a rapid and then fade from view. Dad pulled her out of the water.

'Where's Vlad?' he asked.

'He's up the creek,' Judy told him breathlessly. 'Round the bend.'

'Yes, Judy, I know that,' said Dad patiently. 'I didn't ask you *how* he was, but *where* he was?'

'No, Dad, seriously, he got carried downstream by the current, he disappeared round that bend there.'

Dad hooted with laughter.

'You mean Vlad's gone up the proverbial creek without the proverbial paddle? Didn't I say there'd be trouble if he was let out of his cage?'

'Dad, come on,' said Judy. 'We must hurry further downstream and see if we can find him. Look, that path there, it runs alongside the river. Quick, we may already be too late.'

So they ran along the path as fast as they could, looking in the water as they went.

'Maybe he managed to catch the branch of a tree

or something,' panted Judy.

'He may have been eaten by a fish or dashed against the rocks,' said Dad. 'I bet he wishes he was safe and warm and dry in his cage at this very moment.'

Suddenly Judy stopped and cried, 'Look, Dad, there he is!'

'Where?' said her father. 'All I can see are some people fishing.'

'There, on the end of the rod of the boy in the red bathing trunks.'

'Ha!' said her father, laughing. 'So it is, Vlad caught by a fisherman by the seat of his pants. Before we rescue him I must take a photo of this moment to preserve Vlad's posterior for posterity.'

Dangling at the end of the fishing rod, looking

surprised, wet and bedraggled, Vlad caught a glimpse of Dad with the camera.

'Don't!' he yelled at Dad, but it was too late, the camera went click.

As Dad and Judy approached the bewildered fisherman, Dad called: 'Vlad, I thought you enjoyed having your picture taken.'

'Not with a fish hook in my knickers I don't,' said Vlad huffily. 'Now please get me down from here; I feel a right idiot.'

'Is he yours?' asked the fisherman.

'Not exactly,' said Dad, 'but we're sort of taking care of him.'

'I couldn't figure out what was on the end of my line,' said the fisherman, 'I'm not used to fish shouting "Help" and "Get me out of here". Lucky for you, Vlad, I was fishing just there or you'd have gone right over the waterfall.'

'Ugh,' said Vlad, covering his face with his hands at the thought. 'Snatched from the jaws of death. What a narrow escape. What can I do to repay you?'

'Could I just have a photo taken with you?' asked the boy. 'I could show it to all my mates at school, they'll be really envious.'

So Vlad posed on the boy's shoulder and then they set off back to the others.

'Are you all right, Vlad?' asked Paul. 'I had a terrible shock when I saw you fall out of the canoe.'

'Of course I'm all right,' Vlad informed him. 'I saved the situation with my usual flair and inventiveness. There was nothing to worry about.'

'I'm beginning to see why you kept Vlad in a cage,' commented Aunt Louise.

The next day Aunt Louise took them on a sightseeing tour of Canberra. She drove them round the lake to see the law courts and the art gallery. Vlad moaned non-stop.

'Who cares about boring old law courts and art galleries?' he complained. 'I'm fed up walking round big buildings and sitting in the car. It's too hot. I want to go home. Poor old Vlad, poor little Drac.'

'It's no fun going around with Vlad,' said Judy.

'We'll leave him at home next time,' said Dad.

'That would suit me,' said Vlad. 'I can continue with my researches into endangered species, instead of looking at boring buildings with boring people'

'All right,' sighed Aunt Louise. 'I give in. We'll go back to the house. I'll just drive you round State Circle and you can see the new Parliament House.'

'Can't we just go back?' groaned Vlad. 'It's so hot and I bet that Parliament building is really boring.'

'Be quiet,' said Dad, 'or it's back into the cage with you.'

So they drove round State Circle and the Stones looked at the huge new Parliament House carved into the side of a hill with a huge tower rising up above it, crowned with a vast flag.

'It's very big, isn't it?' commented Vlad. 'What's it for?'

'It's where Parliament meets, where all the politicians who govern Australia meet to debate and pass legislation.'

'Oh,' said Vlad, 'would they be the people who'd pass legislation about endangered species?'

'Yes, I suppose they would,' said Aunt Louise. 'Why?'

'Oh nothing,' said Vlad. 'I just wondered.'

After that Vlad stayed behind most days and practised playing the piano and made notes on endangered species. Each day the Stones went somewhere different and each day they asked Vlad if he wanted to come.

'We're going off to have a barbecue in a nature reserve today,' Judy told him. 'It's a place called Tidbinbilla. You don't want to come, do you?'

'Yes,' said Vlad, closing a book. 'I think I've been overworking. A day off will do me a power of good. I'll come with you.'

'All right,' said Judy, a bit surprised. 'I'll put a bar of soap for you in the Esky, on condition you don't flavour all our food with it again.'

'That was an accident,' Vlad told her. 'It won't happen again, never fear.'

When they got to Tidbinbilla they went and looked at an amazing variety of exotic birds and saw a lot of kangaroos and wallabies jumping around. Dad kept a firm eye on Vlad to make sure he didn't hop into any pouches, but Vlad just looked and made notes and asked questions.

'What are those dirty things?' he asked. 'The ones that look like feather dusters on skinny legs?'

'Those are emus,' Aunt Louise told him. 'There will be lots of them round the picnic site. They're very greedy.'

'They could do with a good wash,' said Vlad disapprovingly.

After looking at the animals for a couple of hours, they went to the barbecue site and began to stoke up a fire. Mum and Paul put sausages and hamburgers on the barbecue and Aunt Louise began to wrap potatoes in tin foil. Judy handed her Vlad's bar of soap and she wrapped that in foil as well.

'That way it will keep all its flavour,' she told him, 'and it won't bother anyone else.'

'Good on yer,' said Vlad, 'that's a bonzer idea.'

'You're picking up strine then, Vlad?'

'I most certainly am,' Vlad told her. 'There are so many misunderstandings otherwise. In fact, I've started keeping a book called *Vlad's Book of Strine*. It's getting quite full. Is my soap ready yet? I'm starving.'

'Give it another minute or so,' said Mum.

Vlad sat and waited patiently. Eventually Mum picked up the bar of soap and was just about to hand it to Vlad, when an emu intervened and snatched the soap in his beak and swallowed it whole.

Vlad looked at the emu in horror. He could see a lump in the emu's throat, where the soap was gradually moving down towards his stomach.

'He stole my soap!' yelled Vlad. 'Did you see that? He just snatched it and ganneted the lot in one swallow. Give me back my lunch, you rotten emu.'

'Nick, go and wave a stick at the emus,' said Aunt Louise. 'None of us will get any lunch if we don't drive them away. It's not good for them to eat our food: their digestions aren't used to it, but they'll steal anything if you give them a chance.'

'That rotten dusty old emu,' moaned Vlad. 'I've just checked on my list and they're not an endangered species, which is a pity since they have such bad manners and greedy ways. Now, what am I going to have for my lunch?'

'Emu steal your tucker?' asked the neighbouring family.

'No,' said Vlad, 'he stole my food.'

'Tucker is food,' said Aunt Louise. 'Yes, he took Vlad's bar of soap.'

'We've got some soap,' said the boy. 'Would you like to have that instead?'

'Thanks,' said Vlad.

So the second bar of soap was grilled and everyone made sure the emu didn't get anywhere near. Vlad ate his soap as the others munched away on hamburgers and sausages.

'Very nice,' he commented. 'Very good tucker.'

The time in Canberra passed quickly and each day Vlad and Dad would practise. Vlad played the piano and Dad the violin.

'The concerts begin fairly soon,' Dad told Aunt Louise. 'So we have to get a bit of practice in. We start performing in Melbourne next week.'

'I shall miss you when you're gone,' said Aunt Louise. 'But I go back to work, so I expect I'll be too busy to notice.'

'What's your job?' asked Vlad.

'I'm the head teacher of a primary school,' she told him. 'We go back next Monday.'

'We don't leave till Tuesday,' Vlad reminded her, 'so that evening we'll do the cooking and have the supper ready when you get back.'

'Thanks,' she said. 'That will be nice, because it's going to be a hard day. I'll be one teacher short.'

'Madam,' said Vlad, 'there is no problem. I am a first rate vampire teacher and I will take the class for one day.'

'Be a relief teacher, you mean?' asked Aunt Louise.

'Exactly,' replied Vlad. 'And why not? A day with a vampire teacher will be a new experience for most of the children.'

'Can I come, Vlad?' asked Judy. 'I'd love to see you teach.'

'Of course,' replied Vlad. 'Who knows, you might even learn something.'

So the next week Judy and Vlad went to school with Aunt Louise. She took them into the class and introduced them.

'Good morning, children. Welcome back after your

137

long holiday. Now, as you know, Mrs Phillips isn't coming back till tomorrow, so today as a special treat you have a different teacher. Children, may I introduce my great-niece, Judy, who is visiting from England, and Vlad the Drac from Transylvania, who is going to take the class. All right, Vlad, I'll leave you to it.'

'Right!' said Vlad. 'All sit up straight. That's better. Now you are all to call me sir and we are going to work very hard today. Anyone who messes around gets vampirised on the spot. Any questions?'

'No, sir,' chorused the class.

'Good,' smiled the vampire. 'Now I am going to test your ability with adjectives. We'll go round the class and each one will have to give an adjective that describes a vampire beginning with a different letter. All right, we'll begin here with the letter A.'

'Vampires are adorable,' said a girl.

'Quite so,' said Vlad. 'Good.'

'Vampires are beastly,' said a boy.

'Think again, son, and think fast,' said Vlad menacingly. 'I didn't come here to be insulted. Come on quickly or you'll get vampirised.'

'Vampires are beautiful.'

'You're getting the idea,' nodded Vlad.

'Vampires are cuddly.'

'Vampires are dinkum.'

'You tired of life or something, sonny?' demanded Vlad fiercely.

'No!' said the terrified boy. 'Honestly, sir, dinkum isn't a bad word.'

'What does it mean?' demanded Vlad.

'It means honest, sir,' the children told him.

'Oh, that's all right then,' said Vlad grinning. 'More strine. I'll have to put it in my *Book of Strine*. Next one now.'

Soon they had a list: vampires were adorable, beautiful, cuddly, dinkum, exciting, far out, great, happy, intelligent, jolly, kind, likeable, matey, nice, organised, pretty, quiet, reasonable, sensible, tolerant, unreal, vegetarians, wonderful, xcellent, yummy, and zany.

Vlad wrote the list on the board.

'Yet,' he told the children, 'in spite of all these excellent characteristics, vampires are in danger of extinction. For the rest of the day we are going to look at other creatures in danger of extinction. Get into twos and I will give you all the name of an animal. Then you must go off and draw it, write what it eats, where it lives and why it is in danger of extinction. Then we will put all the work up on the back wall and give your teacher a surprise when she comes back tomorrow. There is to be no talking loudly, no messing around and no sloppy work. You all know what to expect if you don't do as you're told. The revenge of the vampire is indeed terrible.'

At the end of the day Aunt Louise came in to see what had been going on. The class was silent and on the wall at the back was a huge display entitled 'Endangered Species'.

'Did you do all this in just one day?' she asked.

'Yes,' chorused the children.

'Oh, well done,' she said, 'and good on yer, Vlad. You certainly are a good teacher.'

'Yes,' said Vlad modestly, 'I definitely am, but I enjoyed it and I think the children did too. Didn't you, little ones?'

'Oh yes, sir,' chorused the children, but when the bell rang they ran off home as fast as they could.

10

UP THE POLE

'Didn't you think I was very good with all those children?' Vlad asked Judy, as he sat on her lap on the plane to Melbourne. 'Don't you think I'm the greatest vampire teacher of all time?'

'You were very good,' she assured him. 'And let's hope you do as well performing with the orchestra as you did with the children.'

'Course I will,' said Vlad breezily. 'I'm a very good pianist and I've been practising. Where are we going to stay in Melbourne, Mum?'

'Sir Tibor has found us a place again,' Mum told him. 'He says that as we're looking after Vlad for him, we should have special treatment.'

'I don't see why,' said Vlad looking puzzled. 'I don't see why at all; it's not as if I'm any trouble.'

At the airport Sir Tibor met them and took them to their house. Vlad told him all about the adventures he had had since Sir Tibor had last seen them. When Sir Tibor heard about 'Avoid the Vampire' and 'Vampire Only Day' on the waterchute and the tents collapsing and Vlad drinking the petrol, he roared with laughter.

'Ah, Vlad, my friend, I am so glad you are here. Not only are you a great musician, you are also a great comedian.'

'Appreciation at last,' sighed Vlad contentedly. 'Someone who really understands me.'

'One Transylvanian to another,' said Sir Tibor. 'Now here we are at the house and I will leave you to get settled in. Tomorrow, Nick and Vlad, I will see you for our first rehearsal.'

After that Dad and Vlad went off to rehearse each day and Mum and the children went down to the beach.

'It's very peaceful without Vlad,' commented Paul.

'Yes it is,' agreed Judy, 'but it's a bit boring. At least Vlad and Dad have stopped quarrelling all the time. I'm so glad Vlad is rehearsing every day. He's so tired at night he just flops into his drawer.'

'I know,' agreed Paul. 'And Dad says Vlad is a bit scared of Sir Tibor and isn't messing around at rehearsals.'

'All sounds a bit too good to be true,' commented Mum.

On the night of the first concert, Vlad wasn't performing but decided to go along anyway. He sat quietly in Judy's lap and listened. When the performance was over Vlad clapped loudly and shouted 'bravo' and 'encore' even more enthusiastically than the rest of the audience. The concert was a big success and the next day the newspapers carried excellent reviews. Vlad read the reviews out to the family over breakfast. Suddenly he shrieked.

'There's an advertisement in here for my concert. Listen to this: *Come and hear Vlad the Drac, the world famous vampire pianist, give his first ever concert performance in the Southern Hemisphere on February 10th in the Concert Hall. This rare and special event is to raise funds for endangered species.* Well, what do you think of that?' asked Vlad proudly. 'I shall have to practise very hard to be worthy of my fellow endangered species.'

'If you go on like this, Vlad, I shall have to give away that bird cage,' Dad told him.

141

When the day of the big concert arrived, Vlad put on his brand new penguin suit and bow tie and went off with Dad.

'See you at the concert,' he called to Mum and Judy and Paul, as he and Dad drove away.

'Don't worry,' yelled Judy after the departing car. 'We'll all be there.'

Judy was just putting a comb through her hair when the phone rang.

'Oh, hello, Dad,' said Judy. 'No, no, Vlad isn't here. Oh, he can't have! Oh no! Whatever will you do? All right, we'll get over as soon as we can.'

'Mum,' called Judy, 'that was Dad. He says Vlad has disappeared and they can't find him anywhere.'

'It doesn't sound like Vlad to disappear just when he's got an audience all lined up.'

'And,' said Paul, 'for once he seems to be really concerned about something other than himself. I mean, he really does seem to be genuinely worried about all the endangered species.'

'Dad wants us to get over there as fast as possible and help in the Vlad hunt.'

'I'll stay here in case Vlad comes back or rings up,' said Mum.

When Judy and Paul arrived at the Concert Hall, Sir Tibor and the orchestra were all sitting around looking gloomy.

'What will you do if he doesn't turn up?' asked Judy.

'We'll have to play without him and offer the audience half their money back, if they want it,' groaned Sir Tibor. 'How can he do this to me? When I catch up with him I'll wring his neck. Nick, you should never have let him out of his cage. This vampire, I think he is a little bit crazy.'

'There you are,' said Dad triumphantly, 'at last

142

someone agrees with me. I've had to put up with this sort of thing for the last six weeks. Now you know what it's been like.'

The hall began to fill up with people. The audience were buzzing with excitement at the prospect of hearing Vlad playing the piano. The hall was packed; not a single seat was empty.

'Maybe Vlad will turn up at the last minute,' suggested Judy. 'It's the sort of thing he'd do, just to get attention.'

But the time went on: twenty past seven; twenty-five past seven; half past seven. Sir Tibor put his watch away, gave a deep sigh and said, 'Ladies and gentlemen of the orchestra, let us go and face the public. I will make an announcement that Vlad has been delayed and let us pray to God that he turns up late. First, we will play the ballet music: the audience always enjoys that. After, we'll have to do a little bit of improvisation.'

From the auditorium came shouts: 'We want Vlad!' 'Why are we waiting?' and 'Bring on the vampire.'

'Oh well,' said Sir Tibor. 'Here we go, like Christians to the lions.'

So the orchestra went on stage and sat down, looking very apprehensive. Sir Tibor held up his hand for silence.

'Ladies and gentlemen,' he told the audience, 'our guest performer, Vlad the Drac, has been unavoidably delayed. We hope very much, very much indeed, that he will blow in at some time during the performance. Meanwhile we will play you the ballet music from Swan Lake, Act 2. Forgive, please, the late appearance of our vampire friend.'

This announcement was greeted by cries of 'Shame!' Sir Tibor raised his baton and the orchestra began to

143

play. The minutes ticked by.

'Still no sign of Vlad,' Judy whispered to Paul. The music began to get louder, and a trumpeter put his instrument to his lips and blew hard. A moment later Vlad was propelled out of the trumpet and landed on the drum, just as the drummer was banging down his drumstick with great force. Vlad shrieked and flew away only to be trapped in the cymbals as they were clashed together. Looking dazed, he fell away from the cymbals and fell against the triangle just as the player banged it sharply.

'Help!' yelled Vlad.

The audience roared with laughter and clapped and cheered. Sir Tibor was so surprised to see Vlad emerge from the trumpet he just carried on conducting. Vlad, looking battered, flew over to Sir Tibor just as the conductor brought his baton down hard and Vlad got thumped on the back.

'Stop!' shouted Vlad and he flew over to Dad who was concentrating very hard on playing his violin and didn't see the vampire coming. As Vlad landed on Dad's shoulder, Dad's bow shot up and poked Vlad in the tummy. The crowd laughed and laughed.

'More, more!' they cried.

Vlad caught sight of Judy and Paul sitting in the front row and trying not to laugh. He flew over to Judy and buried his face in her dress.

'Save me!' he cried. 'They're trying to kill me.'

'Shh,' she said. 'Stay here, I'll look after you. It was an accident. Wait till the music is over.'

When the piece was over the audience went wild and Sir Tibor asked Vlad to come and take a bow. Vlad huddled on Judy's lap and shook his head.

'Get everyone to put down their instruments,' she whispered to Sir Tibor. 'I think Vlad's a bit scared.'

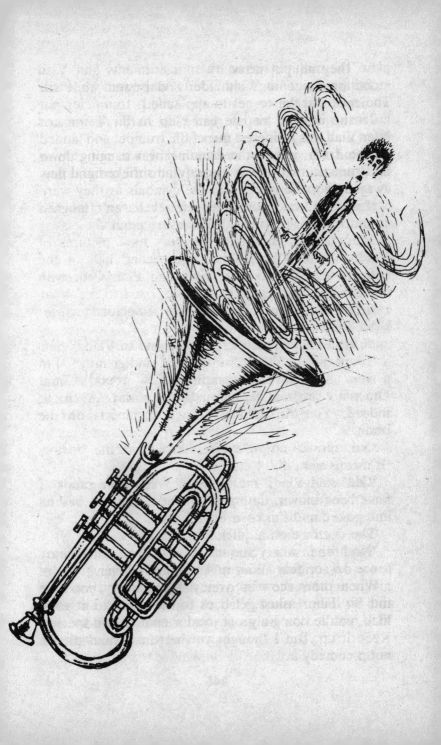

So they all put down their instruments and Vlad stood on Sir Tibor's shoulder and bowed while the audience and the orchestra applauded.

In the interval people came up to Sir Tibor and Vlad and congratulated them.

'What a good idea, pretending he was not coming and then putting all the comedy into the programme. A really good laugh.'

'Inspired!' said someone else. 'I haven't laughed so much for ages. It was worth every penny.'

Journalists from the newspapers took pictures of Vlad and Sir Tibor. When the second half of the concert was due to start Judy and Paul went with Vlad to his dressing room.

'I feel awful,' he told them. 'Call a doctor.'

So a doctor was summoned.

'Sorry to hear you're crook,' he said to Vlad.

'I am not a crook,' said Vlad indignantly. 'I'm a very hard-working vampire. I fly round Count Dracula's castle at least four times a day. A crook, indeed. You Australians have got convicts on the brain.'

'No, crook, not *a* crook,' explained the doctor. 'It means sick, ill.'

'Oh,' said Vlad, 'more strine. Well, I am crook. I have been blown, thumped, crushed, bonked, bashed and poked and I'm covered in bruises.'

The doctor took a quick look at him.

'Nothing to worry about,' he said. 'Just take it easy for a day or two and you'll be fine. I believe you're giving another show in Sydney. Don't worry, you'll be fine by then. I must get back to the concert but good luck, you're doing a great job for endangered species. Keep it up. But I thought you were a serious pianist not a comedy act.'

146

'I am,' said Vlad sourly.

'Are you going to do the same act in Sydney? The audience certainly enjoyed it here.'

'You must be joking,' said Vlad indignantly. 'If you think I'm going to be bashed, bonked, crushed, thumped and poked, just to give a bunch of people a good laugh – ho, ho, ho, ha, ha, ha – you have got the wrong vampire!'

'How did you get inside the trumpet anyway?' Judy asked him after the doctor left.

'I was taking a scientific interest in the various instruments of the orchestra and how they worked. I merely took a little walk up the trumpet, when suddenly snap and I'm locked in the instrument case. I shouted to be let out but no one heard. So I went to sleep. I was awakened by the sound of music but I was stuck inside the trumpet until that idiot blew me out. People! Honestly, I give up.'

The concert was a big success and after that the orchestra moved on to Sydney. Judy was put in charge of looking after Vlad, so that the events of the Melbourne concert were not repeated. Vlad was no trouble; he spent a lot of time practising and, in between, read up on endangered species. Two days before the concert Vlad told Judy he was tired and was going to sleep. Judy put him tenderly in his drawer and tiptoed out leaving him to sleep. The next morning she went to wake him up to give him a tube of toothpaste for his breakfast, when she found to her horror that he wasn't there. She told Mum and Dad, who immediately rang Sir Tibor. He said he'd come over right away. The Stones and Sir Tibor sat round the breakfast table and tried to decide what to do.

'This time I'll definitely wring his neck,' said Sir Tibor. 'It is too much to do this to me twice.'

'We should have left him in the cage,' growled Dad. 'Now, Judy, are you sure Vlad gave you no clues as to where he might be going?'

'No, Dad, he said he was tired because he'd been working so hard.'

'Something tells me that Vlad's disappearance is connected with the endangered species,' commented Mum. 'Vlad's been taking all that very seriously.'

'But if that is the case, where would he go?'

'I don't know,' said Mum. 'I suppose we'd better listen to every news broadcast; we may get a clue.'

So they sat anxiously round the television listening to every bulletin. Judy went into her bedroom and listened to the radio. Suddenly she burst into the front room.

'They've found him!' she shouted. 'He's at the top of the flagpole on Parliament House.'

'Up the pole,' yelled Dad. 'What have I been saying for years? That Vlad is up the pole; now everyone can see that I was right.'

'But I do not understand at all,' said Sir Tibor. 'Whatever is that crazy vampire doing at the top of the flagpole?'

'He is saying he wants to talk to the Prime Minister about endangered species and he wants all Green Australians to come to Canberra to support his stand for species threatened with extinction.'

'We'd better go to Canberra as soon as possible,' cried Sir Tibor, 'and get Vlad down from his pole and back to Sydney in time for the performance tomorrow night.'

'I'll ring and book plane tickets,' said Dad. 'He's a menace, that vampire.'

Dad picked up the phone and dialled around.

'It's hopeless,' he told the waiting group. 'It's the

same story everywhere. Every flight to Canberra is booked out.'

'Try the railway station,' said Sir Tibor. However they got the same answer there, every train solidly booked.

'We'll have to drive,' said Sir Tibor. 'Come on, Nick, Judy and Paul, we don't have a moment to lose.'

'We should be there in four hours,' Dad told Sir Tibor. 'Once you're out of Sydney the roads are good and straight.'

But as they got out of the city they found that the traffic was jammed bumper to bumper and that most of the cars were covered with stickers saying things like 'Save Tasmania's Forests', and 'Don't Log the Rainforests', and 'Keep Australia Nuclear Free'.

'It's all the conservationists,' said Judy proudly. 'They're all going to Canberra to support Vlad. Isn't that good? One little vampire getting all those people to rally to protect their heritage.'

'He chose a very bad time to do it,' grumbled Dad.

Eventually they got to Canberra and parked the car and made their way to Parliament House. All around were huge crowds carrying conservationist banners. At the top of the flagpole above the huge Australian flag was a tiny green speck.

'There he is,' yelled Judy. 'There's Vlad!'

'I bet he's just loving this,' muttered Paul. 'Look, TV crews from all over the world and tens of thousands of people. Vlad's dream come true.'

'Do you know what is happening?' Sir Tibor asked a TV cameraman.

'The PM is going to take the lift halfway up the flagpole and he's going to try and persuade Vlad to come down. Vlad says he'll only talk to the

149

PM himself. A cameraman is going up with the PM. Vlad insisted.'

'I bet he did,' muttered Paul.

'It's going to be broadcast live,' said the cameraman. 'I'm going over to that hotel to see it. Do you lot want to come along?'

So they went to the hotel with the cameraman and there on the screen was the Prime Minister standing on the ledge halfway up the flagpole.

'Hey, Vlad!' called the Prime Minister. 'Can you hear me?'

'Hearing you loud and clear,' replied Vlad. 'Roger and out.'

'You're getting me into a lot of trouble, you know?' shouted the PM. 'What will the Opposition say about me being halfway up the pole and talking to a blood-sucker? I'll never live it down. What do you want me to do?'

'I want you to agree to host a world conference to discuss protecting endangered species and to try and give the conference world wide coverage.'

'All right, I'll do that,' promised the Prime Minister. 'Now, will you come down, so that Canberra can get back to normal? Every road in the city is blocked. Will you come down, please?'

'Too right I'll come down,' shouted Vlad. 'It's very boring up here. Here I come.'

A little later Vlad emerged sitting on the Prime Minister's shoulder and the crowd cheered. Someone gave the Prime Minister a microphone.

'I've agreed to hold a world conference,' he told the crowd, 'to discuss ways of helping endangered species and I hope, Vlad, you'll come to Australia for this conference and give us your views on the matter. You will be the only threatened species to speak. Now, ladies and gentlemen, I'm going to let Vlad talk to you himself.'

The crowd cheered. Vlad grabbed the microphone.

'G'day, you bonzer bunch of fair dinkum Aussie cobbers,' he cried. 'I don't want to give you lot an earbashing but, my oath, I'm not coming the raw prawn when I say you'd have to be a ratbag or a drongo not to rumble that Aussies really care about animals. I'm glad I decided to stop whinging and stick my beak in on behalf of endangered species, because I've got all you lovely greenies with me. Now say with me "I'm green and I'm beautiful".'

'We're green and we're beautiful,' yelled the crowd.

'Right on, cobbers,' Vlad called back to them. 'Good on yer.'

'Well, that's the biggest audience Vlad is ever likely to get,' said Dad. 'Now we'd better go and find him.'

Eventually they tracked Vlad down in the Prime Minister's office. They were ushered in and there sat Vlad on the Prime Minister's desk sipping a cup of hot window-cleaning fluid and chatting to the Prime Minister. When the Prime Minister saw the group he stood up and held out his hand.

'G'day, come on in. I expect you're looking for Vlad here.'

'Hello,' said Vlad brightly. 'Hope you weren't worried but I had to do my bit for the endangerd species.'

'What do you mean not worried?' shouted Sir Tibor. 'We were crazy worried, Vlad. This time you are going back in a cage. No more will I tolerate this disappearing all the time.'

'Oh, don't be hard on him, Sir Tibor,' said the Prime Minister. 'He was only doing what he thought was right and you can't blame a man, eh, I mean a vampire, for that.'

'I'm sorry, Prime Minister, I beg your pardon shouting in your presence, but we were so worried. This is not the first disappearance, you see.'

'So I hear. Vlad has been telling me all about it. We've had an interesting talk, Vlad and I. I've never met an endangered species before, so it's been quite an education for me.'

'The Prime Minister suggested that I might like to come and live in Australia with the family,' Vlad told them. 'Isn't that nice of him?'

'Must be crazy,' muttered Dad.

'But Vlad,' said Judy. 'you'd be so far away, we'd hardly ever see you.'

Dad's eyes lit up. 'It's a wonderful idea,' he said enthusiastically. 'Prime Minister, if you want a truly multicultural society then you must have a vampire colony, otherwise you'd be missing out. Vlad, I think those of us who live in Europe should be self-sacrificing and unselfish and encourage you to complete the rich tapestry of Australian society.'

Vlad swelled with pride. 'You really think Australia needs us?' he asked.

'Oh, definitely,' said Dad. 'No doubt about it. One hundred per cent.'

'We'd love to have you,' said the Prime Minister.

'I shall have to discuss it with Mrs Vlad and the children,' mused Vlad. 'You see, we vampires are very attached to the Carpathian mountains and Transylvania; it's been our habitat for so many centuries. I don't know if I could bring myself to leave it. We are like the Aboriginal people, we are very attached to our ancestral homes. But I will think about it, I most certainly will, and I deeply appreciate the offer.'

'Prime Minister, please excuse me for interrupting,' said Sir Tibor, looking at his watch, 'but we must get back to Sydney for the concert tonight and we have to drive because all the flights are booked.'

'No worries,' replied the Prime Minister, 'I'm going to the concert myself and we can all go in my special plane. So how about a spot of lunch in the restaurant here and I can continue my efforts to persuade Vlad to come and live in Australia.'

So they all went and had a splendid lunch with the Prime Minister. When they had nearly finished the Prime Minister stood up and said, 'Ladies and gentlemen, I would like to propose a toast: please raise your glasses to the preservation of endangered species and to Vlad the Drac, hopefully soon to be the very first Australian vampire.'

While Vlad grinned broadly they all raised their glasses.

'To the preservation of all endangered species and Vlad, the first Australian vampire,' and no one said it with more verve and enthusiasm than Dad.

JOSIE SMITH
by Magdalen Nabb

Collect all the colours of the rainbow with Josie Smith's seven rainbow-coloured books!

Josie lives with her mum. She is resourceful and independent and always does what she thinks best, which often lands her in trouble.

MONTY THE DOG WHO WEARS GLASSES

MONTY BITES BACK

MONTY MUST BE MAGIC

MONTY – UP TO HIS NECK IN TROUBLE

MONTY AHOY!

by Colin West

Monty's glasses are supposed to remind him to look where he's going, but they don't seem to work very well. He has a habit of landing in trouble, whether it's chasing the cat next door, falling in the custard or pinching sausages. But whatever happens, Monty, the dog who wears glasses, always manages to come out on top!

Human beings are a funny lot!

SIMON AND THE WITCH
by Margaret Stuart Barry

Simon's friend, the witch, is loud and outrageous and has a mean-looking cat called George. She behaves atrociously and can't help showing off, but she has a book of spells and a magic wand – and she's the best friend Simon has ever had.

THE MILLIONAIRE WITCH
by Margaret Stuart Barry

The witch has lost her pension book so there's no money for her and no food for George, her long-suffering cat. Simon suggests she gets a job and she tries lots of different things – even singing outside the Town Hall with her friend the Tramp. Then Granny Grim dies and leaves the witch something in her will. Something that will make her a millionaire!

SIMON AND THE WITCH IN SCHOOL
by Margaret Stuart Barry

When the witch discovers she has lost her magic touch, Simon has the answer: "You'll just have to come to school and learn to read." But, once in the classroom, the witch is too busy causing chaos to learn much.

DIMANCHE DILLER

by Henrietta Branford

When Dimanche is orphaned at the tender age of
one, Chief Inspector Barry Bullpit advertises for
any known relative to come forward. Unluckily for
Dimanche, her real aunt does not see the message –
but a bogus one does! So Dimanche, who is heir to
an enormous fortune, is sent to live with the
dreaded Valburga Vilemile, who tries to rid herself
of Dimanche at every opportunity. Her lack of
success owes itself to Polly Pugh, who looks after
Dimanche, foils all attempts to polish her off, and
helps her find her true aunt.

In 1995, *Dimanche Diller* won the Smarties 7-9
category Fiction Award, a prize awarded for the
year's most exciting piece of children's fiction.

Order Form

To order direct from the publishers, just make a list of the titles you want and fill in the form below:

Name ....

Address ....

....

....

Send to: Dept 6, HarperCollins Publishers Ltd, Westerhill Road, Bishopbriggs, Glasgow G64 2QT.

Please enclose a cheque or postal order to the value of the cover price, plus:

UK & BFPO: Add £1.00 for the first book, and 25p per copy for each additional book ordered.

Overseas and Eire: Add £2.95 service charge. Books will be sent by surface mail but quotes for airmail despatch will be given on request.

A 24-hour telephone ordering service is available to holders of Visa, MasterCard, Amex or Switch cards on 0141- 772 2281.

Collins
An *Imprint* of HarperCollins*Publishers*